Meant

to Be

By

Graysen Morgen

2015

Meant to Be © 2015 Graysen Morgen
Triplicity Publishing, LLC

ISBN-13: 978-0996242912
ISBN-10: 0996242910

This is a work of fiction. Names, characters, places, and incidents are the product of the author's imagination and are used fictitiously. Any resemblance to actual persons, living or dead, business establishments, events of any kind, or locales is entirely coincidental.
Printed in the United States of America
First Edition – 2015

Cover Design: Triplicity Publishing, LLC
Interior Design: Triplicity Publishing, LLC
Edited by: Mamie Stevenson and Lauren Weiler, Triplicity Publishing, LLC

Also by Graysen Morgen

Acknowledgements

Special thanks to Lauren and Mamie for catching my mistakes and pointing out my repetitious habits, and to all of those involved with Triplicity Publishing.

To   the avid readers who message me, email me, comment on my Facebook page, and so on: I wouldn't be publishing my thirteenth book if it wasn't for you. Your excitement for each new book and enjoyment of every story are the words of encouragement that push me to write every single day, so thank you all!

Dedication

To my partner, the person who stands beside me as my wife, the mother of my child, and my best friend. Without her, I wouldn't be the woman that I am today.

Chapter 1

Brandt parked her white convertible Porsche against the curb and stepped out, straightening her suit jacket as she headed up the sidewalk towards Roast Me, one of the hottest coffee shops in Los Angeles. She pulled the phone from her pocket, feeling the buzz of an incoming text message. Looking down at the screen, she shook her head. She was on her way to a production meeting at B2, pronounced B squared, the film company she owned with her best friend.

"Damn it," she growled, quickly typing a reply.

Brandt didn't realize she was near the door until someone rushed out of it, bumping into her and pouring a cold cup of iced coffee all over the front of her pantsuit and blouse.

"Fuck!" Brandt screeched.

"Oh, my God," the woman gasped, holding the empty cup in her hand. "I didn't even see you."

"Yeah, sure," Brandt sneered, looking from her stained clothing to the woman in front of her.

"You were coming in the wrong door," the woman said. "This is the exit."

Brandt ran her eyes over the athletic body of the woman. She was dressed in tight, black yoga pants and a black sports bra with a sleeveless, white t-shirt over it that was cut short. The muscles of her stomach were showing from her belly button to the top of the pants. Her light brown hair cascaded in loose waves and curls over her shoulders and down her back, and a pair of white sunglasses covered her eyes. Brandt swallowed the lump in her throat. It didn't matter how good looking the young woman in front of her was—Brandt was still beyond pissed. She checked her watch, shaking her head as she turned to walk away.

"Weren't you going inside?" the woman asked, looking up at the taller woman with short, messy, platinum-blonde hair and dark sunglasses.

"I think I've had all the coffee I want today, thanks to you!" Brandt spat as she stormed off.

The woman shook her head and watched the blonde walk away, before going back inside to replace the coffee she'd splashed all over the stranger.

~

The B2 office was down the street from the coffee shop and Brandt lived out in Santa Monica, a half-hour away, so she didn't have time to go home and change before the meeting. She sneered a few obscenities as she parked in her usual space and walked inside.

"What happened to you?" the receptionist, Renee, asked with an odd expression.

Brandt ignored her. "Do I have any messages?" she questioned as she passed by her.

"Nope."

Brandt set her briefcase on her desk and headed down the hall to the conference room, where her best friend and business partner, Bean Pratt, was waiting for her, along with the screenwriter for a new film prospect.

B2 was a lesbian-only film company where Brandt was a screenwriter and producer, and Bean was a director and producer. They made all of Brandt's movies, along with a number of other screenwriters' stories, and so far, they had been very successful.

"I know I'm late. I ran into a situation," Brandt said, stepping into the room and taking a seat at the table.

Bean pushed her dark-framed glasses up on her nose and furrowed her brow at the disheveled woman next to her. "What happened to you?" she asked. "You smell like Starbucks."

Brandt looked at her best friend. Bean was quirky with shoulder length brown hair and big brown eyes. She'd always reminded Brandt of Tina Fey with her nerdy looks and odd sense of humor.

"Some girl spilled her coffee all over me," she sighed.

Bean laughed, "Only you."

"You must be Francesca," Brandt said, extending her hand to the woman across the table. "I apologize. My morning hasn't gotten off to a good start."

The dark-haired woman smiled. "It's no problem, and please, call me Fran. I'm happy to be here, and if it's any consolation, I think you smell divine."

Brandt laughed.

"I was going to have Renee bring some coffee in, but I think we can all catch an espresso buzz off Brandt," Bean laughed and continued. "Fran, you're here because we took a look at your script and think it has potential."

"I was confused by Paola's character at first, but by the end, it all comes together. Your story touches on the push and pull of a lesbian who is in a relationship with a bisexual woman. This has been done numerous times, but no one has ever written it from both sides with such emotional drama," Brandt said.

"We've only made true lesbian movies, so this would be a first for us," Bean added. "But we both feel like you have a great story...and..." Bean looked at Brandt. "We'd like to produce it, with a few adjustments of course."

"Wow," Fran exclaimed. "Yes. This is great!" She smiled brightly. "What are the changes?"

"The scene changes need to be stronger and there are a few blocking issues, but other than that, we should be good to go," Bean replied.

"Wonderful. When can we get started?" Fran asked.

Bean smiled. "We have a lot of paperwork to take care of first, then we'll go through the script to make sure we've corrected everything. After that, we'll storyboard it, and once we're ready to move forward, we'll begin set building and costumes. At that time, we'll also start casting."

Fran nodded. "Where will you film it?"

"We have the rights to a studio lot in Vancouver. We film all of our movies on the lot and on location in the surrounding city," Brandt answered.

"Sounds great." Fran smiled.

~

After the meeting, Bean went into their company attorney's office to draw up the contract for the screenplay while Brandt went into the film room to work with the person who was editing and sound mixing her latest picture.

"Viv, how's it going?" Brandt asked, sitting down next to the red-haired woman in front of the four large computer monitors.

"You stink!" Viv replied, wrinkling her nose.

Brandt growled, "I know!"

"Check this out," Viv said, pointing towards the headphones lying on the desk. "I merged the dream scene with the end of the first kiss like Bean wanted, and then I added the first track of the guitar solo."

Brandt nodded and put them on as she watched the middle screen and listened to what Viv had done. The scene lasted about three minutes, but it was powerful and a turning point in the story.

"This is great!" Brandt exclaimed, removing the headphones.

"Sweet. I'm going to paste this in and move to the end. We have about fifteen more minutes to edit and then we'll be finished with the rough cut."

"Already? We just wrapped two weeks ago."

"I know, but it's coming together. What can I say? When you're good, you're good!" Viv teased. "I'll have it ready to screen next week." She grinned.

Brandt smiled and shook her head before walking out of the room and heading to her own office. She really wanted to go home and take a shower, but she had too much to do. She looked at the framed picture sitting on the corner of her desk. Brandt was dressed in a dark pantsuit and holding a glass of champagne. Her arm was around the waist of a gorgeous woman standing next to her, who was wearing a purple cocktail dress with her ash-blonde hair falling over one shoulder.

"Has it sunk in yet?" Bean asked from a few feet away as she walked further in, taking the seat across from Brandt at the large desk.

"What?" Brandt said. She hadn't heard Bean enter the room and was slightly startled by the sudden voice.

"You're getting married in two weeks!"

Brandt smiled, looking at the picture of herself with her fiancé one more time. "I'm not nervous, if that's what you're asking."

"Are you sure you want to be off the market?" Bean teased.

"I've been off the market for the past three years," Brandt laughed.

"How's Jenna?"

"Fine. She's in New York for her final dress fitting."

"I still can't believe she chose a wedding planner and dress maker in New York City. You live in California!"

Brandt shrugged. "She lived there for a number of years, so she knows a lot of people, especially in the fashion industry."

"I guess being a model and an actress has its perks," Bean stated.

"Who knows," Brandt replied. "Viv showed me the dream scene. That came out nice."

"Yeah, we worked over the weekend on a few more merges. It's coming together."

"She said the rough cut will be ready to screen soon."

"Yep, and now we're moving on with Francesca Diamante's screenplay."

"I think this story is well-written, and it should be a hit, but I don't want to completely open up to the bisexual industry. It's all over the damn place when it comes to movies and books."

"Yeah, no doubt. I agree a hundred percent. If this story had a different ending, you can bet your ass we wouldn't be making it," Bean replied. "Besides, we're getting ready to move forward with your next project anyway. As soon as you come back down to Earth from the wedded bliss orbit you've been stuck in."

Brandt shook her head and laughed. "I feel like my head is spinning in so many directions. I think I've seen Jenna all of two weeks in the past three months. I'll be glad when the wedding is over."

"Oh, the life of two lesbian superstars," Bean teased.

"Kiss my ass, Bean," Brandt chuckled.

"So, what actually happened to you this morning?"

"Oh, my God." Brandt shook her head. "I was replying to your text when this chick plowed into me. The lid popped off the cup of her iced coffee and I basically took a bath in it."

"Wow!" Bean laughed hysterically.

"It wasn't funny at the time and I'm sure my shirt's ruined. I hope it comes out of this suit. I just bought it."

"Did she apologize?"

"No! The bitch blamed me for going in the wrong door!"

Bean shook her head. "What she at least hot?" she giggled.

"No, yes…I don't know. I barely looked at her. I was so angry, I'm sure I had smoke coming from my ears."

"What did she look like?"

"A yoga instructor," Brandt laughed. "I didn't stand there and have a long conversation. I was pissed and I walked away. She was cute, I guess, but she's an asshole. I'm getting married— you do remember that, right? I'm not really looking at other women."

"Well, I'm single!" Bean exclaimed.

"Bean, you're single because you divorced the dragon you married. Be happy you're not in that situation anymore. Besides, I know for a fact that your sheets are never cold!"

"Yeah, that's because they think I'm that damn actress."

Brandt laughed and looked down when her phone lit up with Jenna's picture.

"The future Mrs. Coghlan is demanding your attention," Bean teased as she stood up to leave.

Brandt answered the call as Bean was walking out the door.

"Hey."

"Brandt, the florist just sent me a picture of the bridal bouquet and it's horrible. She said something about the flowers blooming late and having a problem finding what I asked for. I need you to go straighten it out."

"Why didn't you talk to her?"

"I'm in New York!"

"What's wrong with what she sent you?"

"It's ugly as hell and it's nothing like what I ordered!"

Brandt sighed, "What do you want it to look like?"

"Brandt, we discussed what we wanted all of the flowers to look like. You don't remember?"

"I wasn't with you when you ordered them, so I have no idea what they're supposed to look like!"

"White roses, white orchids, and white calla lilies with blades of grass. She has pink roses and some kind of purple leafy shit in there. It's hideous and not at all what I wanted."

"I'll call her. When are you coming back to L.A.?"

"I have my fitting this afternoon, then Tiffany and I going to get the bridesmaid gifts, and finalizing the music after that. If everything is fine with the dress, I'll be home tomorrow night. Otherwise, I'll need to stay until it's correct."

"Alright, send me her number." Brandt knew her bride-to-be was a perfectionist and she couldn't fault her for that, but she was starting to sound more and more high-maintenance as the wedding neared. She looked over at the picture on the corner of the desk and was reminded why she'd asked Jenna Harte to marry her in the first place. She was beautiful and both of their careers had started to soar once they became an item. They enjoyed each other's company, and when Brandt had won her first award as a screenwriter, Jenna was next to her. She'd felt like she had everything she could ever want or need in that moment, and she'd proposed that night.

"Let me know when you've straightened out the florist."

"Send me a picture of the dress."

"No!" Jenna chided. "You can't see it until the big day."

"You picked out what I'm wearing and you were there for the fitting."

"That's different. I have to go. I'll see you soon, babe."

Brandt ended the call and waited for Jenna to text her the florist's info.

Chapter 2

A week later, Brandt and Jenna were walking out of Samurai, an upscale sushi restaurant, when a young man asked to snap a few photos of them for *Out Magazine*. Brandt and Jenna were becoming the new lesbian power couple. They smiled and walked to Brandt's car. She held the passenger door open for Jenna, before going to the driver's side and sliding down into the leather seat of her sports car. Her eye caught the skin of Jenna's upper thigh as the mini dress she was wearing rode up. Brandt grinned and started the car.

"Dinner was good," Jenna said, looking through the window as Brandt drove. "I didn't care for that new roll you ordered though."

"I thought you liked whitefish."

"I do, but not with the sweet sauce in that roll."

Brandt nodded and slipped her hand from the gearshift to Jenna's bare thigh. "I missed you while you were in New York."

"I missed you too." Jenna smiled, squeezing Brandt's hand. The large diamond on her hand sparkled under the interior lighting.

Brandt removed her hand to downshift for a red light, and Jenna moved her own hand to cover the spot where Brandt's had been. Brandt didn't bother moving it back. She knew they'd both been stressed out lately—Jenna over the wedding and Brandt over her latest film. With Brandt traveling back and forth to Vancouver and Jenna back and forth to New York, they had barely seen each other in the past couple of months, and even then it was mostly in passing.

"One more week and hopefully things will go somewhat back to normal." Brandt smiled.

"What do you mean by that?"

"After the wedding, you won't be traveling to New York and I have a month or two before we start filming our next picture, which isn't mine. Therefore, I won't be on set the whole time anyway. We'll finally get some time to slow down."

Jenna smiled. "I don't think I remember what that's like."

"You will as soon as we get onto that cruise ship." Brandt grinned.

"The best part about getting married is definitely the honeymoon," Jenna agreed.

When Jenna's phone made a noise indicating a text message, Brandt asked whom it was out of curiosity.

"Tiffany. She has a question about the venue," she said, texting her back.

Brandt nodded and turned into the gated community where she lived in the Santa Monica Mountains. She drove up the street and pushed the button to open the gate for the driveway, before parking in the garage next to Jenna's Audi.

"I'm not going to stay over tonight. I don't know if it was dinner or if my period is coming. My stomach is cramping," Jenna said, wrapping her arms around Brandt's neck.

"That sucks. You don't have to leave because you don't feel well. This will be your house too after next week."

"I know." Jenna smiled. "I love you. I'll call you tomorrow."

"Let me know if you need anything," Brandt said, walking Jenna to her car. "I love you, too." She kissed Jenna's lips softly, lingering with their bodies pressed together.

~

The rest of the weekend had gone by in a blur for Brandt. Jenna had started her period and wasn't in the mood for anything but her TV remote and a pair of sweatpants, so Brandt had spent all of Saturday and well into Sunday morning, in her home office, working on her new screenplay. She'd finally drug herself out of the house Sunday afternoon to go buy a couple of new shirts and a bathing suit for the honeymoon cruise to Mexico. Then, she'd stopped at Jenna's to bring her the dinner she'd picked up before heading home.

~

On Monday morning, Brandt sat at the island in her kitchen, drinking a glass of fresh juice she'd made in the juicer she and Jenna had received as a wedding gift the week before. She'd been trying different combinations of fruits and vegetables and decided cucumber and carrots with a slew of mixed berries seemed to taste the best. It had also given her a little bit of extra energy, so she'd started drinking it every morning.

She stood in the doorway of the kitchen, looking out over the open floor plan of her living room. She wasn't used to living with anyone. In fact, she hadn't lived with anyone since she moved out of her mother's house at eighteen years old to go to film school. She'd bought her land after the first movie she'd written and B2 produced. Then, a year later, she worked with an architect and designed the modern styled house she'd always pictured in her dreams. After Saturday, Jenna Harte-Coghlan would be living in that house as her wife; Brandt would have to compromise and more than likely make a few changes.

She finished her juice and rushed up the stairs to get ready to go into the office. She left with enough time to stop at Roast Me on the way. It was the closest coffee shop to her office and it was the best by far. She hadn't been back since the mishap, which subsequently cost her a blouse and a hefty dry-cleaning bill, but she wasn't avoiding the café for that reason. She'd simply been too busy to stop on her morning drive lately. Between the wedding, her film that was being edited, the screenplay she was working on, and Fran's screenplay, she barely had time to sleep, much less take an extra ten minutes to get great coffee. The one downside to Roast Me, was the fact that it was walk-in only. They didn't have a drive-thru and, they didn't have room to build one either.

~

Brandt looked in all directions and made sure she was on the right side as she stepped near the door. The barista recognized her and smiled.

"Caramel mocha?" she asked.

"Yes, ma'am," Brandt replied.

"You haven't been here in a while."

Brandt smiled. Obviously, the young woman hadn't seen the disaster the week before. "No, I've been busy, in and out of town."

"I see," she said, sliding the hot cup of coffee across the counter.

Brandt paid her and grabbed the cup, taking a long sip before she walked out. She'd drank a third of the medium-sized cup by the time she got into her car and drove off. The office was only a block away and Bean was getting out of her BMW when Brandt pulled in next to her.

"You're taking your wardrobe into your hands going back in there," Bean teased. "Did you see your nemesis?"

"No, thank God. I went in, got my usual, and left with no problem."

"You got lucky." Bean shook her head and smiled. "Are you nervous yet?" she asked, bumping shoulders with her as they walked inside.

"No. I think I'm more grouchy about having to give up half of my house," Brandt said honestly.

Bean laughed. "Jenna's going to completely redecorate and expect all of her crap to come with her."

"Ugh," Brandt sighed. "Don't remind me. I mean, I love her, but she has a cat and her furniture doesn't match mine. My house is fully furnished. There's no room for her crap, or the cat."

"You should've thought of this before you put that rock on her finger."

"We love each other and I'm sure we'll make it work," Brandt replied as she opened the door to her office.

Bean shrugged. "I like Jenna, she's hot and she's not a bad actress, but she's smart and I can guarantee she'll have you redecorating your house as soon as you guys return from your honeymoon."

"Care to make a friendly wager?" Brandt asked.

"Sure," Bean said, stepping closer. "I have a hundred bucks that says you're redecorating."

"Make it a thousand," Brandt replied.

"Cash only," Bean snickered, holding her hand out to shake on it.

"Deal!" Brandt shook back and stepped into her office.

"Hey, Viv wants to go over the credits and fonts this morning. She needs to get them in today."

"Okay," Brandt stated and checked her watch. "An hour?"

"Sure."

Chapter 3

On Friday, Brandt walked into the B2 office as usual. She set her briefcase on her desk and walked down to Bean's office.

"What are you doing here?" Bean asked with a raised eyebrow. "This is your last single day, girlfriend. You should be living it up."

"I'm getting a haircut this afternoon and picking up my tux after that. I don't have anything else to do. I might as well work."

Bean shook her head. Since you wouldn't let us throw you a bachelorette party, we'll find something else to do. Viv has the rough cut of the movie ready. Let's go screen it and call it a day."

"It's eight-thirty in the morning."

Bean laughed. "Come on."

Brandt followed her down the hall to the screening room.

"Hey, I didn't expect to see you until tomorrow," Viv said. She was dressed in skinny jeans and a tight '80s style t-shirt that didn't help her shapeless figure. She was built like a flat stick. Her short, dyed red hair stuck out in all directions, making her look a lot younger than the tender age of forty-three.

"She came to see the rough cut, then we're all taking the day off to party!" Bean exclaimed.

"Awesome!" Viv high-fived Bean.

"I didn't say that," Brandt added.

"I'm your best woman and she's your grooms woman or whatever the hell you call it, so we're in charge," Bean replied.

"Wonderful." Brandt shook her head and grinned.

Bean and Brandt sat down on the couch in front of the large screen with notepads in their hands and Viv went to start the movie, returning to sit next to them once it was going. Brandt was on the edge of her seat when she was watching one of her own movies. She'd been doing this for ten years, but it still gave her an adrenaline rush and made her want to puke at the same time. The thrill of watching something she'd written on paper or a computer screen come to life before her eyes was the highest of highs.

Brandt made a few notes as she watched the 85-minute film. When it was over, Viv jumped up to shut it off and Bean turned to her.

"Well?"

"I have a couple of things I want to change with the music and the editing of the fight scene. Other than that, it's great." Brandt smiled.

"I think we have another hit on our hands," Bean added.

Viv returned and Brandt told her about the subtle changes she wanted to make. Viv took the notes to the editing room and left them near her computer, then she walked to the front of the office building.

"I'm going to drive back to Brandt's to drop off her car and change clothes, then we'll meet you at Oliver's for a late lunch," Bean said to Viv.

"The martini bar?"

"Yes. They have a kickass lunch menu," Bean replied.

"Alright. See you at one?"

"Sounds good."

"We have too much work to do for everyone to take the day off," Brandt asserted.

"Wait a second," Bean ran back inside. "Renee, turn the machine on an take the rest of the day off. We'll see you tomorrow at the wedding."

"Are you sure?" Renee asked.

"Yes. All you'll be doing is answering the phone. If we get any packages they can put them in our drop box or wait until Monday. Tell the rest of the staff they can leave early too. Enjoy your day and lock up on your way out!" Bean said, before running back out to the parking lot. "I'm going to stop at home to change into jeans. I'll be at your house in an hour."

Brandt nodded and got into her car.

~

Oliver's Martini Bar was hopping with a late lunch crowd. Brandt wasn't surprised since it was Friday afternoon and most of L.A. seemed to take three-day weekends. It was the last weekend in March and the weather was in the sixties with clear skies. She was dressed in jeans, a mint green button-down oxford-style shirt with three-quarter sleeves, tucked into her jeans with a thick brown belt and brown loafers with no socks.

The host showed them to a high-top table in the bar, where their waiter was standing. Viv ordered the first round of martinis while Bean perused the menu, finally settling on a couple of sampler platters from the appetizer list.

"Here's to Brandt's last day as a single woman!" Bean said, holding her drink up to toast when the round of martini's arrived at their table.

Brandt laughed and raised her drink, along with Viv. They clinked their glasses and took generous sips of the vodka beverages.

"You guys are nuts, you know that, right?" Brandt teased.

"Yes, but you love us!" Bean replied.

"Uh huh." Brandt grinned.

"What time is your haircut?"

"Five o'clock, and I have to get my tux by seven."

"No problem," Bean said.

~

They were about to order their second round of drinks, after blowing through the appetizers when Brandt's phone rang. She looked down at Jenna's smiling face on her caller ID.

"Hey, babe."

"Where are you?" Jenna asked. "The answering machine is picking up in the office."

"Oliver's. Bean surprised me with a day off to celebrate and Viv joined us."

"The martini bar?"

"Yes."

"Maybe I'll come up and celebrate too," Jenna replied.

"Cool. Love you." Brandt hung up the phone. "That was Jenna, she's coming up here."

"I thought this was your last day of freedom party. Don't you think your bride-to-be shouldn't be here?"

Brandt shrugged. "She didn't want to see me before the wedding, so this is a surprise too."

Bean nodded and Viv ordered another round.

Jenna walked in twenty minutes later, wearing a dark blue one-piece jumper that had full-length pants with a halter-style top, and black high heels. Brandt stood from her stool and kissed her lovingly. Jenna, who was already two inches taller than Brandt, towered over her in the heels.

Viv moved so Jenna could sit next to Brandt at their square table.

"What are you drinking, babe?" Brandt asked.

"Dirty Goose with two olives," Jenna said to the waiter.

"You sound like a martini girl." Viv smiled.

"A little bit." Jenna grinned.

Bean ordered more appetizers when the waiter returned with Jenna's drink.

"So, this is what a Friday afternoon is like at B2 Pictures," Jenna teased.

"Don't we wish," Viv replied.

"Right," Bean laughed, toasting her.

"I thought you weren't going to see me until tomorrow?" Brandt asked.

"Tiffany had a Skype meeting with another client in New York, so she's back at her hotel. We're meeting with my bridal party to go over the last minute stuff in an hour. We finished everything else a little while ago, which is why I had time to see you."

"Are you sure we didn't need another rehearsal?" Brandt asked.

"The one we did last night was fine, at least it looked like it to me," Bean added.

Jenna smiled at her. "I agree," she said, grabbing Brandt's hand.

Brandt leaned over and kissed her, lingering a little longer than normal because of her buzz. Jenna grinned and kissed her again.

"I'd say get a room, but you're getting married in twenty-four hours, so I guess a little PDA is acceptable. Damn love birds," Bean teased.

~

They had another round before Jenna left to go meet with the wedding planner and her bridal party. Brandt looked down at her watch. It was after six.

"Fuck!" she exclaimed.

"What's wrong?" Viv asked.

"I missed my haircut and the tux place is across town. I'll never make it before seven and they close at seven-thirty. Son of a bitch!" Brandt swayed slightly. Four martinis didn't usually make her buzz this bad, but all she'd eaten was a couple of small plates of appetizers.

Viv had stopped at two drinks and Bean had given her third to Brandt.

"Call and see if you can do it in the morning. The wedding isn't until three o'clock," Bean replied.

"Yeah."

"I'll see you guys tomorrow. I need to get home and feed my mutts," Viv said. "I had a great time."

"Me too," Brandt replied, hugging her goodbye.

"We should probably go too. I'm sorry we lost track of time," Bean stated.

Brandt called and left a message with the woman who cut her hair, saying she had an emergency but she'd be in there at noon. The reason Brandt had wanted to get her haircut the night before was because her hairdresser was working the late shift the next day. She placed a call to the tux rental shop and told them she'd be there when they opened at nine in the morning to pick up her tux.

When Bean dropped her off, Brandt went straight to the shower and then to bed. She woke up around two a.m. and worked on her screenplay for about two and a half hours before going back to sleep.

Chapter 4

Brandt woke up at nine the next morning surprised she wasn't hung over. She dressed quickly and hurried out of the house, arriving at the tux store at ten.

"You look like it's your wedding day," the man behind the counter said when Brandt handed him the pink receipt.

She grinned. "Possibly."

He smiled and walked to the back, returning a few minutes later with a white garment bag.

"There's a changing room to the right. Go ahead and put the shirt, jacket, pants, and shoes on to make sure they fit okay. Also, check the tie and vest colors to make sure they're correct."

"No problem," Brandt said, disappearing around the corner.

She removed her jeans, sneakers, and long-sleeved shirt, setting them to the side. Then, she unzipped the bag and pulled the white pants from the hangar. They fit great in the waist, but were a little too long, even with the shoes on. She shook her head and buttoned the smooth, white dress shirt, which fit perfectly. Then, she pulled the white jacket on and looked in the mirror. She'd never seen herself in all white and it looked slightly odd. She peaked into the bag at the satin necktie and matching vest. They were the same platinum color she and Jenna had ordered. She was more of a bow tie person than neckties, but that's what Jenna had wanted her to wear. She also owned a very nice, and expensive, custom-made black tux, but Jenna wanted them both in white for their wedding day. She'd lost that argument as well.

"How is everything?" the man said from the other side of the door.

"The pants are too long," Brandt replied.

"Is everything else okay?"

"Yes. The shirt and jacket are perfect."

"Step out and I'll see what I can do," he stated.

Brandt sighed, checking her watch as she walked out of the room.

"Hop up on the podium. Oh, I see. Yes, definitely two inches too long." He shook his head, then looked at the shirt and jacket. "Alright, let me get my pins."

Brandt watched as he moved to the other side of the room and returned with sewing pins. She held still while he made an adjustment to the pants and pinned them in place.

"Okay, carefully take these off. Those pins will get you if you're not careful. It'll take me about an hour to get these sewn up."

Brandt nodded and changed back into her regular clothes. He was already dealing with another customer when she walked out.

"My assistant will be here in a little bit, and then I'll get your pants fixed. Is this a good number to call you at?" he asked, looking at the paperwork.

"Yes. I have another appointment at noon, so I'll be back after that," she replied.

She had a half hour to get over to the hair place, which thankfully, was close by. She slid into her car and pulled out into the traffic. Her stomach was growling, but she didn't have time to stop.

When Brandt arrived at five minutes to noon, her hairdresser was sitting in her chair.

"I got your message," she said.

"I'm sorry, Jules. My best friend and bridal party decided to take yesterday afternoon off and go to a bar. I completely lost track of time."

Jules laughed. "It's no big deal."

"I'm paying for it today, though. I was supposed to pick up my tux last night too, and when I tried it on this morning, my damn pants were way too long. The guy is fixing them now, so I'm supposed to come back after this."

"What time is the wedding?"

"Three. I have to be at the venue by two o'clock," Brandt sighed.

"You're cutting it close."

"Yeah, no kidding."

"So, we're just doing the regular trim, right?"

"Yes," Brandt answered.

Jules sprayed some water in Brandt's hair and began combing her short tendrils that stuck out in all directions.

"You know, most women pay hundreds of dollars a month to get this beautiful platinum colored hair that you have naturally, and you chop it all off!" Jules laughed.

"I love long hair, just not on me." Brandt smiled. "The shorter the better."

"You know, your hair has a natural wave. It bet it would be beautiful long."

"Yeah, well, that's too bad."

Jules laughed and began trimming her hair. "So, what bar did you go to?"

"Oliver's."

"Is that the upscale martini bar?"

"Yeah. I've been there a few of times," Brandt replied.

"Is it worth the money?"

"I drank four martinis and was on my ass. That doesn't usually happen."

Jules laughed. "I'll have to check it out. That sounds like my kind of place, although I'm not much of a martini drinker."

"I'm not either, but Jenna likes them. So, we've gone there a couple of times."

~

As soon as Brandt was finished with her haircut, she hurried back over to the tux shop.

"Your pants are ready," the man said with a smile when she walked in.

Brandt rushed into the room and tried them on. True to his word, the pants were hemmed perfectly. She quickly changed back to her jeans.

"Thank you so much."

"Congratulations," he replied with a smile as she rushed out the door.

Brandt set the tux bag in the passenger seat of her car and walked around to the driver's side. She needed to be at the venue in 30 minutes and it was all the way out in

Santa Monica Beach. She started the car and pulled out into the traffic, cutting over quickly to take a side road that would hopefully lead to less traffic.

A couple of blocks away, she stopped at a red light and BAM!

Someone smashed into the back of her.

"Damn it!" she yelled. Her head hadn't whipped forward too much, so the person wasn't going extremely fast, thankfully, but nevertheless, she was rear-ended by someone who obviously hadn't been paying attention.

The first thing she noticed was her car engine was no longer running. She turned the key a couple of times, trying to start it so she could move out of the road, but it wouldn't turn over.

"Fuck!" she exclaimed, getting out of the car.

A small, dark purple Mercedes SUV was smashed up against the back of her car. She could tell the engine compartment of her Porsche was damaged, which was why it wouldn't start.

"I'm so sorry. I didn't see the light change," a woman said, getting out of the SUV.

Brandt looked up at the woman dressed in loose fitting gym pants, a sports bra, and a cut-off tank top. She caught a small glimpse of some kind of writing tattooed down the woman's right side. Her light brown hair was twisted up haphazardly in a loose bun with a few curly tendrils falling down on her shoulders.

"Oh, you've got to fucking be kidding me! You! You're the one who hit me?" Brandt sneered, recognizing the young woman from the coffee shop who had poured coffee all over her a couple of weeks earlier.

"Great," the woman said, shaking her head. "Are you at least okay?"

"I'm fine," Brandt growled," but my damn car won't start."

"I'm really sorry."

"What were you doing? Texting?" Brandt snapped.

"No. A bug flew in the window as I was braking for the red light and I flipped out trying to get it away from me. The next thing I know, BAM!"

Brandt shook her head. "Seriously? All of this for a goddamn bug?"

"I'm allergic to bees and wasps!"

"Great," Brandt sneered as she pulled out her phone and pressed Bean's name.

"I've already called the cops."

"Yeah, well, don't expect them to get here anytime soon and I'm not worried about the damn cops. Today is my wedding day and now, instead of being excited and happy, I have to get my damn car towed and find a ride so I can make it to the fucking venue on time! All because of a bug!" she yelled.

"Hello? Brandt?" Bean said into the phone.

"Hey, sorry. Can you come get me?"

"You're not at the gardens?" Bean asked. "I'm about to pull in there."

"Hell no. Some dumbass just rear-ended me."

"Oh, my God. Are you okay?"

"Yes, I'm fine, but my car won't start. I need you to hurry up and come get me. I need to go call the insurance company so they can send the tow truck."

"Alright. Where are you?"

"I'm on Charleville in Beverly Hills, east of Santa Monica Boulevard."

"What are you doing way the hell out there?"

"Picking up my damn tux!"

"Are you sure you're not hurt?"

"No, I'm fine. Hurry up."

As soon as she hung up with Bean, Brandt called her insurance company, who promptly called a tow company for her. Then, she called Jenna to let her know what had happened, but she got her voicemail, so she left a simple message.

The cop finally showed up when the tow truck arrived. He looked at both cars and shook his head. "You're blocking traffic. I need you to pull into that shopping center over there," he said.

"I'd be glad to, but my car won't start."

He raised an eyebrow and looked at the white Porsche again. "Why won't it start? You were rear-ended."

"The engine is in the back," Brandt said, making him look like an idiot. "Look, the tow truck is here. Why don't you go ahead and let him take it?"

"That's fine," he replied.

Brandt went over to the tow truck driver and gave him her information. He told her the insurance company instructed him to tow it to the closest Porsche dealer, which she agreed. Then, she took all of her stuff out and watched him load her car onto the flatbed.

The other driver's car started and ran fine. The front bumper was dented in pretty good, but it was still drivable. The cop had her drive it over to the shopping center and Brandt rode with him over there.

Brandt got out of his car and leaned against the side while he wrote the other driver a ticket. She had stayed in her car, which was fine with Brandt. She'd had two run-ins with this woman and no matter how sexy she looked in her gym clothes, or how perfect her body was, Brandt wanted to smack her head off her shoulders. She checked her watch again just as Bean pulled into the parking lot.

"That's my ride. Can I go? It's my wedding day, literally in forty-five minutes."

"Sure. You can look up the ticket information on our website. Congratulations," he said.

Brandt rushed over to Bean's car, where she tossed her tux bag and other stuff into the backseat.

"Can you believe this shit?" she growled, sliding into the passenger seat.

"That car doesn't look too bad."

"Yeah, well, my motor is in the back of mine."

"Oh, I forgot about that," Bean replied, pulling out of the parking lot.

"You're never going to guess who hit me."

"Britney Spears."

Brandt laughed, "No."

"Jennifer Anniston."

"She lives in New York, I think."

"I don't know. One of the Kardashian's?"

"Nope. The chick from the coffee shop who drenched me a couple weeks ago."

"No shit!"

"No shit," Brandt said, shaking her head.

"Maybe it's fate. You said she was cute."

"I'm getting married...in 30 minutes."

"I'm just saying. Everything happens for a reason. What's she look like, by the way?"

"She's beautiful. A little shorter than me, maybe a couple of inches, but she has a smoking body, and medium brown hair with honey colored highlights. It's wavy and sort of spiral curly. She was dressed in gym clothes both times, so I think she's a pilates or yoga instructor or something. She definitely has the body for it and she has something tattooed down her right side."

"Interesting. She sounds sexy as hell."

"Yeah, if you're single and like chaos, which is all she seems to cause me."

"She sounds divine. Can I have her number?"

"You can have her, as long as you keep her the fuck away from me. Now, step on it! I can't be late to my own damn wedding."

Chapter 5

Brandt looked at herself in the mirror. The pristine white tux fit her simple curves perfectly, giving her lines a slightly feminine appeal. She wasn't a fan of euro ties or conventional neckties, but the platinum colored tie and vest combo contrasted nicely with the white of the suit and shirt. Bean and Viv were dressed in black suits and white shirts with no tie or vest to go with the black dresses of Jenna's maid of honor and bridesmaid. She'd wanted a very traditional look with an elegant black and white contrast.

"This is it," Brandt murmured to herself in the mirror as she reached for the full champagne glass on the nearby table. She emptied the glass in two long sips and blew out a nervous breath.

A soft knock at the door grabbed her attention. She figured it was Bean and Viv coming to tell her it was time, but a strawberry blonde head appeared, then the rest of the petite body. Brandt cocked her head to the side. Jenna's maid of honor and best friend, Isabel, was standing in front of her in jeans and a t-shirt with an envelope in her hand.

"I found this when I got here a few hours ago. I looked all over before I figured it out," Isabel said, handing Brandt the envelope.

"What?" Brandt replied, pulling the letter from the envelope.

"I'm so sorry, Brandt."

Brandt unfolded the letter.

Brandt,

I care for you so much, and I used to picture myself spending the rest of my life with you. Somewhere in the last year, I lost who I was, and I need to find myself. I need to be Jenna Harte for a while. I've done nothing but focus on being Mrs. Brandt Coghlan, and I don't think that is who I really am, at least not right now. I'll always love you and care for you.

Jenna

Brandt wadded the letter up and tossed it on the floor of the dressing room.

"She took a flight to New York this morning, I'm assuming with the wedding planner. I had no idea. I thought it was odd when she never wanted me to go with her to help with the wedding planning, but…this…I'm sorry," Isabel sighed.

Brandt tossed her empty champagne glass against the wall, shattering it to pieces. Then, she removed her jacket and began loosening her tie.

"Can you go make an announcement please?" Brandt murmured.

"Sure."

~

When Bean found out what had happened, she rushed into the dressing room. Brandt's tux was strewn about, and the waded paper was on the floor near the pile of glass. Brandt was long gone. Bean quickly dialed her cell, but it kept going straight to voicemail because she'd turned it off. She asked Viv to help Isabel handle the situation and return the tux, before rushing out of the venue towards her car.

~

Brandt noticed everything that Jenna had left at her house over the past three years was suddenly gone, and her key and garage opener were lying on the island in the kitchen. She didn't once feel like crying. Surprisingly, she wasn't sad, just extremely pissed. She felt like she'd wasted the last three years of her life and Jenna had made a fool of her in front of their friends and family.

She pulled a bottle of whiskey and a glass from the bar in the living room and walked out onto the pool deck. She plopped down on one of the chaise lounge chairs, pouring herself a glass, before setting the bottle on the small table between the two chairs.

Her house was in the mountains and situated sideways so that her backyard was on the side of the house where a cliff overlooked a small valley with the face of the next mountain behind it. The front of the house had the driveway with grassy areas on both sides of it, as well as the wrought iron fence that surrounded the property. The side opposite the pool housed the three-car garage and the actual back of the house, which was the end of her land, so the wrought iron fence continued around the back to the railing along the overlook next to the pool.

Brandt took a long swallow, trying to calm her angered nerves as she looked out through the railing at the mountains in the distance. This was the last thing she thought she'd be doing on her wedding day as the last three years of her life rolled through her mind like a horribly written movie. Brandt knew she and Jenna had grown apart in the past year while she was in Canada shooting another film, then traveling around the world to different screenings and film festivals for another movie that was releasing. In the past, Jenna had traveled with her, but this year, she'd chosen to stay home and plan the wedding of her dreams.

When Jenna had told her she wanted to go with a wedding planner from New York City, Brandt was confused, but Jenna said the woman was the best, and she named a bunch of celebrity weddings the woman had planned. Brandt agreed and the next thing she knew, Jenna was flying back and forth to NYC every month, on Brandt's dime of course, since she'd taken the year off from work to focus on the wedding.

Brandt heard the doorbell of the house ringing over and over. Figuring it was probably Bean, she turned her phone on and sent Bean a text message saying she was fine and just wanted to be alone. Then, she sent another message saying she'd call her tomorrow, before turning her phone back off.

Brandt shook her head, thinking back to the past three years. She should have known Jenna was whoring around in New York. Jenna knew she was beautiful and she flaunted it everywhere she went. The fact that she was an out lesbian only added fuel to the fire. Men and women had thrown themselves at her on more than one occasion. She was a magazine model and had been in a couple of movies, so she'd become more known each year that they were together— so much so that people were asking to take pictures with her on the street. Brandt had a huge following of her own, but mostly with the lesbian population. She was cute and her movies were extremely popular, winning one award after the other.

Brandt poured another glass and sighed before taking a long swallow. She should've known this was coming instead of being blindsided. She seemed to be on a runaway train full of bad luck. First, the coffee incident, then the car crash, and now she was dealing with the disaster of a lifetime. One thing she was certain of was the fact that she'd never really known Jenna, because if she had, she never would've let the relationship get this far. It definitely wasn't meant to be and she was played like a fool. She was glad Jenna had decided to go find herself before they'd actually said I Do.

Feeling a lonely tear slide down her cheek, Brandt stood and tossed the glass in her hand as hard as she could across the pool, and over the rail, into the valley below. Then, she wiped the tear away as she grabbed the bottle and headed into the house, where she chugged a few more long sips and stretched out on the couch in the living room.

Chapter 6

The next morning, bright rays of the sun splintered through the open blinds of the French doors and directly onto Brandt's face as it rose over the mountains and picked the perfect spot to stop. She stirred a few times, then squinted her eyes open. She nearly rolled off the couch as she tried to get the blinding light from her eyes. Her head pounded like it was being squeezed in a vice as she sat up. The whiskey bottle on the table reminded of her of the bitter reason she was waking up on the couch with a hangover. She sighed and stood up, before heading up the stairs to take a shower and wash away the last twenty-four hours of her life.

After a hot shower and an equally hot cup of coffee, Brandt was starting to feel alive again. She turned her phone on and shook her head at the amount of text messages, missed calls, and voicemails she'd received, before deleting everything without listening to or reading what they had to say.

She headed upstairs to her office, hoping a little bit of work would help clear her mind. Brandt sat at her desk and stretched her arms over her head—that's when she saw the papers sitting on the edge.

"Shit!" she exclaimed, grabbing them as she began searching for a phone number to cancel the seven-night honeymoon cruise to Mexico that she and Jenna were supposed to leave on in six hours.

Finally finding a number, she quickly dialed and pushed all of the menu buttons to hopefully be connected with someone.

"Destiny Cruise Lines. How many I help you?" the man answered.

"Hi, I have a booking for a cruise that is leaving today, and I need to cancel it," Brandt said.

"I'm sorry, ma'am. All sales are final one month before departure."

"Even for emergencies?" she asked.

"I'm afraid so. You can cancel your booking, but you will not receive a refund."

"Well, son of a bitch," Brandt growled.

"Excuse me?" the man exclaimed.

"Never mind," Brandt stated, hanging up. "Looks like I'm going to Mexico," she murmured.

~

The car service had arrived on time as previously scheduled, and after standing in an hour-long line, Brandt was finally aboard the Dream of Destiny cruise liner. She found her way to her suite towards the aft section of the ship, where her luggage was waiting by the door for her. She'd been on a handful of cruises over the years, so she was familiar with how things worked.

"May I help you with your bags, or get you anything?" a woman with a heavy accent asked.

Brandt turned to see her stewardess standing nearby. She had short brown hair and was dressed in the customary steward clothing of black slacks with a white blouse and a vest with the cruise company logo on the left breast.

"I'm fine. Thank you." Brandt smiled.

"My name is Hilda. Please let me know if either of you need anything."

Brandt furrowed her brow in question, then remembered the itinerary was for two people in the suit who were on their honeymoon.

"Actually, it's just me and I'm going to make the best of this trip...alone."

The stewardess nodded and walked away.

"I'm getting off to a great start," Brandt murmured sarcastically as she carried her suitcase into the suite.

Through the door she found a small hallway with a closet to her right and the bathroom to her left. Then, the room opened up into a large area with a king-sized bed on one side, and a couch with two chairs and a table were on the opposite side. The far wall had two large floor-to-ceiling windows and a thin set of French doors that led out to the private balcony. Brandt looked around and smiled, knowing this was going to be way better than she'd expected when she decided to suck it up and go alone. She could've easily taken Bean with her, but she wanted to be by herself and take this week to get over the anger of Jenna's deceit so she could come home and move on with her life.

~

A steel drum band was playing island music when Brandt got off the elevator on the top deck. She bobbed her head as she walked over to the bar near the pool and ordered a piña colada. The blonde bartender winked as she handed over the tall glass full of frozen booze with a pink umbrella sticking out of it. Brandt smiled and pulled the umbrella out, biting off the cherry on the button and chewing on the pineapple, before tossing it in the nearby trash can. She walked over to the rail, watching the people down on the dock as they readied the ship for departure.

She was well into her second drink by the time the ship finally pushed away from the dock and began the slow journey out of the harbor. An announcement was made over the loud speaker for everyone to don their life vests and head to their muster stations for the mandatory safety drill. Brandt rolled her eyes, finished the last of her drink, and headed back to her room to get the bright orange horseshoe-shaped thing they called a life jacket. Her muster station was located in the show theater, so she moseyed down the two flights of stairs to avoid the crowds at the elevators, and walked into the large room. A wine colored curtain was drawn over the wide stage. The room was decorated in gold tones with rows of seating in the middle with individual cup holders on the sides like a movie theater. Large booths with tables were along the back and sides of the room, and the upper floor was laid out in the same fashion with rows and booths.

Brandt walked down to the open booth on the right side of the stage and sat down with a bunch of strangers. As soon as the sound bell sounded, a handful of cruise ship employees walked out onto the stage with life vests in their hands. They were dressed in dark blue pants and shorts with white t-shirts that had the cruise ship logo on the front and the words Entertainment Crew on the back, and sneakers on their feet.

One of the males had a microphone in his hand, which he promptly turned on to begin to address the crowd. The other men and women spread out across the stage so everyone in the room could see one of them. Then, he started going over the safety rules and proper way to where the life jacket, which each of the crew members demonstrated.

Brandt moved to the edge of her seat, squinting through the bright lights and little bit of alcohol she'd had to see the person wearing the orange contraption on her end of the stage. The man explained that once everyone had their jackets on, the next step would be exiting through the back doors and moving down the side hall to the exterior deck of the ship where three lifeboats awaited them. At that point, they'd be put into the boats and lowered down to the water. She vaguely listened as she tried to place the familiar woman on the stage, wondering if she'd cast her in a film.

"You've got to be kidding me!" she growled when it finally hit her.

The entertainment crew member on the stage, playing with the straps of her life jacket and laughing with the other crew members, was none other than her nemesis; the same woman who seemed to be causing her nightmares. She looked different wearing something other than workout clothes and her hair was twisted up in a clip, but Brandt was sure it was her.

"Son of a bitch!" Brandt shook her head, flabbergasted at her shitty luck. The man next to her scrunched his face, looking at her sideways. "Not you, sorry," she said, still shaking her head as she watched the woman.

When the drill was over, Brandt took her life vest off and walked against the crowd towards the stage, where the entertainment staff was climbing down to answer questions and help everyone exit without any mishaps.

Brandt walked directly up to her and said, "I'm doomed if you're the crew member who is supposed to get me safely off this ship!"

The young woman gasped in surprised and swallowed the lump in her throat. The last person she'd ever expected to see on the ship was the hot-headed blonde she kept running into— literally.

She looked around behind the woman, remembering she was getting married and figuring it was probably her honeymoon. "Where's your husband?" she asked.

Brandt laughed at the thought of having a husband when she clearly screamed lesbian.

"The woman who should be my wife right now is in New York finding herself with someone else," she stated.

The young crew member raised her eyebrows in shock. "I'm sorry," she said.

"I'm better off without someone like her and my honeymoon is now a relaxing, fruity-drink-filled vacation for one. Or at least it was until this point."

"Don't worry. I've been working on cruise ships for five years and I've been through thousands of drills, most of which we load and lower the boats to the water per maritime regulations." The young woman smiled thinly.

"That's good to know, but you were trained to drive a vehicle, too, at least well enough to get a license, and look what happened," Brandt added.

"I'm really sorry about your car and I sincerely hope you enjoy your trip, despite the circumstances," the young woman replied.

Brandt was surprised at how polite she was acting and figured she was working, so she must have to kiss all of the guests' asses. She looked at the young woman's eyes, noticing their pale green color for the first time. It was like nothing she'd ever seen before, except maybe on a cat.

She cleared her throat and replied sarcastically, "I will as long as you don't accidentally knock me overboard."

The young woman laughed, "That's not likely."

"What do you do on the ship, besides show people how to wear a life vest?" Brandt asked, still slightly mesmerized by her eyes.

"I'm a dancer and choreographer with the entertainment crew. We're on this stage twice every night and over the course of the cruise, we'll perform five completely different shows. You should come see one of them."

Brandt nodded and smiled. "I might do that."

"As many times as I seem to run into you, you'd think I would know your name by now." The young woman grinned.

"Brandt Coghlan," she said, sticking her hand out.

"Summer Durham. It's nice to actually meet you," she laughed, sliding her hand against Brandt's.

"Yes, it is," Brandt replied.

"Again, I'm really sorry about everything, the coffee, your car, and the runaway bride."

"Thanks." Brandt smiled. "See you around."

Summer watched her walk away, thinking it was going to be a long cruise, and praying she didn't do anything else stupid in front that woman.

Chapter 7

By the time Brandt had made her way back up to the pool deck bar, they were at sea and the state of California was no longer visible on the horizon. She ordered another frozen cocktail and walked to the row of lounge chairs lined up along the aft rail of the ship, where she settled comfortably in one of them, stretching her legs out in front of her.

The warm sun felt good on her skin and the cool breeze smelled like salt and the combustion of diesel fuel from the smoke stack behind her. She stayed in her chair, nursing the drink in her hand as the sun sank behind the clouds.

When the stars finally littered the sky, Brandt made her way back to her room to get ready for dinner. Since it was the first night, she decided to just change from her shorts and t-shirt to a pair of stone colored chinos and a pale yellow polo shirt. She slipped her dark brown Sperry boat shoes on and headed to the dining room.

The large round table was nearly full once Brandt was shown to her seat. The sting of the vacant seat next to her was a slap in the face reminder of why she was on the cruise in the first place. A few people introduced themselves and Brandt did the same. When the head waiter came around to welcome everyone, he stopped to say congratulations to Brandt, who simply smiled a fake smile and nodded. A few people at the table looked at her.

"This..." Brandt said, wrapping her arm around the empty chair beside her. "Was supposed to be my wife, and this was supposed to be our honeymoon, but shit happened and now I'm here on vacation." A few people gasped as she removed her hand and grabbed her water glass. "So, I propose a toast— here's to fun, sun, and moving on over the next seven days!"

"Amen, sister!" one woman yelled, holding up her glass.

"You go, girl!" the friend next to her said.

Everyone at the table began holding up their glasses.

"I think we need something better to toast with than water," one guy exclaimed as he waved the waiter over. "Brandt, what are you drinking?"

"Whatever you're ordering." She smiled.

"Let's have two bottles of chardonnay brought over."

The waiter nodded and disappeared.

~

By the end of the three-course meal, the seven people at the table had finished three bottles of wine and learned more about each other than they'd ever remember. Brandt finally bid them adieu as she headed for the casino. The loud chiming of slot machines rang in her ears when she walked through, looking for her favorite game.

Only two of the four roulette tables were open, so she squeezed into the one with fewer smokers sitting around it and laid two one hundred dollar bills on the green felt.

"Singles or nickels?" the dealer asked.

"Nickels," she stated, indicating she wanted to play with five-dollar chips instead one- dollar chips.

He nodded and stuffed the money down the slot in the table, then slid a small stack of purple and black chips towards her. The people around her were playing singles, so their chips were a plain designed solid color like red, blue, yellow, or green, with white in the middle, whereas the nickel chips were fancier and had a black center with the $5 symbol in white. The quarter chips, which were twenty-five dollars each, were even more intricately designed with a red center and the $25 symbol in the middle. The one hundred dollar chips were simply black with a white center with $100 in red inside of that.

Brandt pulled her stack close and began placing two of her chips, for a straight ten dollar bet each, on six different numbers. There were a hundred different ways to play the board, but the largest payouts were inside betting on the actual numbers, and a straight bet on a single number had the highest payout on the table, so that's what she always played. If a gambler wasn't careful or lucky, he or she could easily lose their stack of chips in only a few rolls of the ball by playing this way. The outside betting, which is black or red, odd or even, or pockets of numbers, is a safer bet with much higher odds, but it has the lowest payout.

Brandt selected: number ten for her birthday; twenty-five for Bean's birthday; thirty-three for her age; two for her favorite number, thirteen because it was lucky for her, and eighteen because that was her botched wedding date. Then, she looked down at the table as the dealer turned the number wheel and spun the ball in the opposite direction. She'd always found it bad luck to watch the ball; instead, she listened to the rolling and looked up when it landed on a number.

"Twenty-five," the dealer said loudly, placing the pointer on top of Brandt's chips covering the number.

"Yes," she cheered, collecting her $350 worth of winnings as the dealer slid a large stack of chips towards her.

When the dealer finished paying everyone who had won, he removed the pointer and opened the table. Brandt placed the same bet as before. The ball stopped on the number one and the only people who had won were those playing the outside. She sighed and ordered another frozen fruity drink before placing her same bet once again.

She lost one more time before hitting on two more numbers, bringing her winnings to a total of $960 after the $120 she lost on the two losing rolls. Take out the $200 she'd started with and she still walked away with over $700. Brandt cashed out and walked away from the casino. She could've easily sat there all night, winning some and losing more, but she had fun playing the game and not losing the money, which is why she only played a little bit.

Checking her watch, Brandt realized she had time to catch the late show in the theater, so she skipped the elevator line and hurried down one flight of stairs and searched for an open seat on the bottom floor. The only open space she could find was towards the back, but nevertheless, she squeezed in.

Brandt had missed the sign at the door presenting the show theme for the night, so she had no idea what she was in for as the house lights went dark. A single spotlight lit the center of the stage as the curtain began to rise, and a few music chords teased the crowd. Everyone cheered when the dancers ran out together in four male/female pairs. The women were dressed in long poodle skirts of various colors and black blouses with white sweaters, and their hair was up in ponytails. The men had on suits with black pants, bright colored jackets that matched the poodle skirt color of their dance partner, and thin black ties. The décor of the stage made it appear like a '50s or '60s era diner.

"Great Balls of Fire" by Jerry Lee Lewis began playing and the dancers dove right into a lindy hop and Charleston swing dance number. Brandt bobbed her head along to the music as she watched the exciting routine.

When the music changed to another '50s tune by Chuck Berry, the women removed their sweaters and met the guys in the center of the floor for a high-energy jive dance of boys versus girls. That's when Brandt realized the woman leading the girls was Summer. She watched closely as the men and women paired up again for a face-paced quickstep routine. She was impressed with the dancing skills of the young woman and realized this was why Summer had an incredibly athletic body.

After the song ended, Brandt found herself clapping with the rest of the crowd as the dancers disappeared back stage. Two different pairs of dancers came out to dance another Doo Wop era dance to a fast song. The crowd watched in anticipation as Leslie Gore's "You Don't Own Me" started and all of the women came out for a female-only troupe number. They'd changed into mock suits that had thin black jackets and white blouses with open collars, showing a bit of cleavage, and loose black neckties. The outfit finished with a short chiffon skirt attached to the bottom. The song quickly changed to "Pretty Woman" and the women, led by Summer, moved into a staggered group of eight and danced multiple routines from the Madison to the Mashed Potato. Brandt cheered when the song ended. The men quickly came out dressed as greasers in leather jackets, white t-shirts, and jeans, and they danced another high-action routine.

The final number of the show started with the men losing their jackets and the women coming out in their same outfits, minus the jackets and ties. Their blouses were tied up at the bottom under their breasts, revealing their bare stomachs, and their hair was down. Each guy grabbed a girl's hand as they broke off into pairs to dance to three different '60s era songs. They started with the rock and roll dance and mixed in modern steps, including a snippet of grinding moves from *Dirty Dancing*, where the men and women were connected at the hips and the women bent over backwards, looking at the crowd upside down, before coming back up to finish the grinding steps. Summer's long, wavy hair swung around as her body twisted and turned. Brandt's eyes were glued to her as the audience cheered loudly with hoots and whistles.

Once the show was over, Brandt walked out of the theater with the mass of people, at which time she noticed the "Doo Wop Night" sign near the entrance door. She took a detour to the stairs at the other end of the deck and headed down one floor to the sing-a-long piano bar she'd noticed earlier that day. The small room was packed and the only open seat was at the bar surrounding the piano. She quickly sat down and ordered a drink from the waitress as she passed by. The piano player had just started the first few lines of an Elton John classic, which Brandt knew well, so she fell right in step with the rest of the people who were singing loudly.

Chapter 8

Brandt finally made it back to her room around two a.m. and rolled out of bed a little after nine the next morning. After a quick shower, she dressed in a t-shirt, shorts, and flip flops. She was about to leave the room when a colored paper on the desk caught her eye.

"Damn it," she huffed, reading the printed information for the two person excursion she had booked for the next day. It was another reminder that the cruise was supposed to be shared with someone else—her wedded wife.

Brandt folded the paper and slipped it into her pocket as she headed out of the room to find something to eat to curb her growling stomach. She stepped into the elevator at the end of the hall and rode up two decks to the dining room, which of course was closed since she'd missed breakfast. She shook her head and walked down one floor to the shore excursion desk on the promenade deck, the same deck as the show theater.

"I'd like to cancel this excursion I'd booked for tomorrow," Brandt said, pulling the paper from her pocket.

The woman behind the desk took the paper and typed a few keys on the computer in front of her.

"Hey, you," Summer said, sliding up next to Brandt at the counter.

Brandt looked at Summer, who was dressed in bright blue warm-up style pants and a white Entertainment Crew t-shirt. Her long hair was hanging in spiral waves down her back and over one shoulder. Her pale green eyes glimmered in the bright lighting of the atrium behind them.

"Do you wear contacts?" Brandt blurted out.

"No," Summer laughed. "How's your cruise going?"

Brandt smiled. "Pretty good, so far. I saw the show last night."

"What did you think?"

"I enjoyed it. I felt like I was watching *American Bandstand* or something," Brandt answered.

"That's what we were going for. I choreographed about half of those dance numbers." Summer smiled.

"Really? It was great. You're an incredible dancer, which is surprising with the klutzy way you walk and drive," Brandt teased.

Summer laughed.

"Ms. Coghlan, I'm sorry. Your excursion is non-refundable," the woman behind the counter interrupted.

"Damn. Are you sure?" Brandt asked.

The woman nodded. "That's the policy."

"I'm sorry," Summer said, stepping away from the counter with Brandt.

"What's your schedule like? Do you do other things besides the shows?" Brandt asked.

"The entertainment staff hosts trivia and bingo games every afternoon in the theater and we split it up, so

I work with that every other day, but I am in both shows every night."

Brandt nodded. "What about tomorrow when we're in port?"

"Thankfully, I'm off until the rehearsal before our first show of the night."

Brandt looked at the woman next to her. The last person on Earth she dreamed of being stuck on a cruise with was the person who had caused her so many problems in the past few weeks, but the woman standing next to her seemed like a completely different person, not to mention the fact that she was beautiful without trying to be. Brandt was almost sure she didn't have a stitch of make-up on. "Do you want to go snorkeling tomorrow?" she blurted without thinking twice.

"What?" Summer laughed.

"Snorkeling. With me. I have two non-refundable tickets for this damn excursion."

Summer raised her eyebrows in a slightly shocked expression. Up until yesterday, the slightly taller woman standing next to her had wanted to punch her out, and truth be told, she'd wanted to smack her back just as bad. "I probably shouldn't," she said.

"I'd actually welcome the company, as long as you don't drown me." Brandt smiled.

Summer laughed and pursed her lips. "Okay, I guess."

"Great. The tickets say to meet in the globe lounge at eight tomorrow morning with your swimsuit and a towel," Brandt informed.

"I'll see you then." Summer smiled. "I need to get to bingo," she said stepping away.

"What's the show theme tonight?" Brandt called after her.

"Psychedelic Night...'70s music. The early show is PG, but the later show is better," Summer yelled.

Brandt walked away with a smile on her face as she headed towards the casino. She hadn't meant to meet anyone on the cruise, and certainly not her nemesis, but Bean always told her everything happened for a reason. She was starting to see the meaning of that statement.

~

The roulette tables were packed, so Brandt sat down at a slot machine long enough to get a drink. She ordered the frozen drink of the day having no idea what was even in it. She blew twenty dollars on the machine before the woman returned with the bright pink drink with a yellow umbrella. Brandt gave her room card to her to add it to her tab, then she ate the fruit and tossed the umbrella in the trash.

She'd nearly forgotten she didn't eat breakfast until her stomach rumbled loudly. Brandt checked her watch and walked over to the craps table. It was close to lunchtime, so she figured she'd just grab something then.

"Honeymoon!" a man yelled from across the casino.

Brandt turned around with a raised eyebrow to see one of her dinner table mates walking towards her with his drink held in the air like a long distance cheers or high five.

"Are you playing?" he asked.

She shook her head and laughed. "Hey. No, not this game. I tend to lose a lot of money on this table."

"Aw, come on. It's fun," he said, stepping up to the table and bending to put two twenty-five dollar chips on the pass line.

Brandt watched as a woman on the other end tossed the dice, rolling a five with the dice on three and two. Brandt watched over the man's shoulder as the shooter tossed the dice again. This time, they landed on seven, mostly known as craps. The man sighed and placed another bet on the pass line. Brandt shook her head and walked away.

The buffet lines were opening in the aft café on the other side of the pool when Brandt arrived. The smell of Mexican food tickled her nose, causing her stomach to growl loudly as she maneuvered into the shortest line and grabbed a plate. There was a choice between hard taco shells and soft taco tortillas, as well as larger burrito tortillas. She grabbed two of the soft taco tortillas and moved along to the meat section, where cooks were making fresh shrimp, chicken, and beef. She asked for shrimp and watched the cook place a handful of large shrimp on each tortilla. Then, she slid over to the topping area, where she added a little bit of lettuce and tomato, and then covered that with sour cream, cheese, and salsa. Feeling satisfied with her lunch design, she stepped away from the buffet bar and sat down at an open table.

Her lunch tasted as divine as it smelled. She ate slowly while watching people meander about. There were so many things to do and see on the ship—it was no wonder people often repeated the same cruise multiple times.

~

After lunch, Brandt headed back to the bar outside of the casino to listen to the karaoke contest. Two women from her dinner table waved her over to where they were sitting.

"Do you sing?" one of the women asked. She reminded Brandt of Wilma Flintstone with her bright red hair and big fake jewelry.

"No," Brandt replied, shaking her head. "There's not enough alcohol on this boat to get me to sing."

"Oh, we'll have you up there," the other woman giggled.

Brandt laughed, realizing they were definitely the Wilma and Betty duo. Although the giggling woman had dyed blonde hair, she was wearing a light blue sundress and had the fakest laugh Brandt had ever heard.

"I ran into your husband earlier," Brandt said to her.

"Oh, Phil...he lives in the casino. You probably saw him losing money at the craps table."

"No, actually, he was winning," Brandt lied, wondering how much money he lost per trip. The group of four seemed to cruise together quite often judging from their dinner conversation.

"Well, that's good news then." She smiled as she went through the song list and circled the ones she wanted to perform.

Once the music began, Brandt sat there long enough to see each of them perform, as well as a handful of other people, before making up an excuse to go to the bathroom. Neither of them noticed her taking the fruity cocktail she was drinking with her.

Back in her room, Brandt changed into a bra-style bathing suit top that was solid blue and switched from panties to the boy shorts bottoms that matched the top. She was fit and trim from going to the gym a few times a week and eating healthy most of the time, and she had subtle curves in the right places. She nodded at herself in the mirror.

"You've still got it," she laughed, before pulling a t-shirt and shorts on over her swimsuit and heading up to the sun deck to soak up some rays for the rest of the afternoon.

Chapter 9

The rest of Brandt's afternoon was spent lounging in a deck chair, listening to the sound of the water churning from the ship's props and the steel drum band playing in the background, while consuming more frozen drinks. As she stared up at the cloudless sky, her mind drifted to Jenna and the events of the last forty-eight hours. Their three years together had been easy from the very beginning when they met on the set of a movie B2 was producing. Brandt hadn't sat in on the casting, so she met everyone on the first day of filming. Jenna Harte was a beautiful blonde model with the bubbling personality and curvy assets to prove it. She and Brandt had hit it off during a conversation about the movie, which was Jenna's first picture. She'd already been in dozens of magazines and a handful of short films, but she was nervous about the large set and trying to keep up with the fast pace. Brandt had seen her for more than the exterior shell that no one seemed to get past. When the movie wrapped, they'd went on a couple of dates and within two weeks had officially become an item.

Thinking back, Brandt couldn't remember ever having a major argument. Most of the time, they went with the flow to please each other, and with their work schedules, they didn't get much time together often, so the last thing they wanted to do was disagree on things.

Brandt wondered if lying there and psychoanalyzing her ended relationship was the best idea. It was over and probably had been over before she'd ever proposed. She just didn't see it because she was too busy being comfortable with the way things were. It sure felt like Jenna had been doing her own thing on the side a lot longer than the spur of the moment note she'd left saying she'd needed to find herself. She'd more than likely found whatever she was looking for a long time ago and didn't know how to tell Brandt.

Brandt thought about the excursion planned for the next day and she couldn't help feeling a little excited. It had been a while since she'd simply let go and had a good time and this cruise seemed to be the perfect atmosphere. She still couldn't believe she'd asked Summer to go snorkeling with her. What the hell had she been thinking? She'd certainly not been drinking, so she couldn't blame it on that.

"I hope she doesn't drown me or get me eaten by a shark," Brandt murmured to herself.

The young dancer was the most naturally beautiful woman she'd ever seen with the face of an angel and the body of a goddess. She'd have to be dead not to feel a physical attraction to her, but the woman was a magnet for disaster, especially where Brandt was concerned.

~

At dinner, Brandt ran into the table mates she'd seen earlier in the day. She'd forgotten all of their names, so she mentally identified them as the Rubbles and the Flintstones.

"Did you win?" she asked, smiling at the man she'd seen playing craps. She referred to him as Barney since he was married to the giggly blonde in the blue dress from the karaoke bar.

"Oh, you know, you win some, you lose some."

Brandt nodded, thinking *not really*.

"What did you do today? We never saw you come back to sing," the red-haired woman asked.

"I laid in the sun. I forgot how relaxing that is," Brandt answered honestly. Analyzing her relationship had actually been more beneficial for her than the sun.

"We're going to the late show in the theater tonight," the other woman mentioned.

"Yeah, I'll be there too. The one last night was great."

"We missed it because we went to the watch the comedy show in the globe lounge," the redhead's husband said.

This was the first time Brandt had heard Fred speak. He usually nodded and went along with everyone else.

"I heard it's a '70s theme tonight," Brandt added.

"Yes, that's why we're going. That show is about the only thing I remember from the '70s," Wilma laughed.

Brandt smiled and watched the other two members of the table arrive late.

"We went back to our room for a quickie," the woman shook her head and laughed. "When you're fifty, they're not quick anymore!"

The Flintstones and Rubbles laughed in agreement and Brandt wanted to crawl under the table and puke. She flagged down the waiter and ordered a double whiskey on the rocks.

"How was your day?" the quickie man asked. "I hope you're still having a good time, despite everything."

"I am enjoying myself, actually. Maybe not as much as some of us." She grinned.

Brandt wanted to say she had a snorkeling date for the next day, but it wasn't really a date. In fact, she didn't know what it was and she didn't really want to put a name on it. Summer was a stranger that she was hoping would become a friend. The last thing in the world she wanted or needed was a relationship with anyone. At this point, she would take a vow of celibacy if she didn't like sex so much. No, her excursion the next day was just that—a fun time with a new friend, nothing more, and certainly not a date.

The waiter brought Brandt's drink and she took a long swallow.

"You know, the best way to get over a woman is to under another one," Fred said.

Brandt nearly spit whiskey all over the table. She was starting to like this Fred more and more. "Well, I'll take that into consideration," she replied with a grin.

~

After dinner, the boat was rocking in rough seas and Brandt went back to her room to change and found an elephant folded out of towels on her bed with a piece of chocolate next to it. Brandt moved the towel animal to the coffee table, keeping it intact. She then changed from her polo shirt and slacks into jeans and a button down shirt, but made the mistake of lying back on the bed for a minute to rest her eyes. She woke up again at one in the morning, cursing like a sailor because she'd fallen asleep. The sun and booze had obviously worn her out. She quickly shed her clothes, opting for a t-shirt and shorts with nothing under them as she stepped out onto the balcony to look at the stars in the black sky.

Chapter 10

The next morning, Brandt ate a little bit of the breakfast she'd had sent to her room and was on her second cup of coffee when she walked into the globe lounge. She didn't see Summer and she still had ten minutes to eight anyway, so she sat in a less crowded area of the room and nursed her coffee. She looked around, not recognizing anyone. It wasn't like her table mates were into anything remotely involving exercise to begin with.

"Is that coffee?" Summer asked, sitting down next to her.

"Yes. I'll toss you overboard if you spill it on me!" Brandt growled with a hint of a smile.

"Are you sure you want me to go snorkeling?" Summer asked.

Brandt shook her head and smiled a little bigger. "If I didn't want you to go, I wouldn't have asked you," she replied, looking at the woman next to her.

Summer's hair was up in a bun and she had dark sunglasses up on her head. She was wearing a loose fitting tank top with the dark purple straps of her string bikini tied behind her neck, and a pair of very short shorts. Brandt looked down at the white flip-flops on her feet and noticed a tattoo around her ankle.

"It's a tattoo anklet made up of music notes." Summer pulled her left leg up for Brandt to look closer.

"That's interesting," Brandt said, looking at the different parts to it.

"It's the first chord of the first song I choreographed a professional number to." Summer put her foot down and pulled her tank top up. "I have this one as well."

Brandt looked at the squiggle marks going down her side in a line from just her breast to the top of her waist. She remembered seeing part of this one at the accident scene. "What does it mean?"

"Live life. It's written in Bengali. I fell in love with the symbolism of the language and 'live life'...well, that's kind of my motto."

Brandt peeled her eyes away from the silky smooth, naturally tanned skin being revealed to her.

"Do you have any tattoos?" Summer asked.

"No. Do you plan on getting more?"

Summer shrugged. "I don't want to be covered in them, but I'd like to get more. My line of work doesn't really allow a lot of tattoos, so that'll probably never happen."

"Welcome to Puerto Vallarta! We have four snorkeling excursions leaving from here," a man dressed in a tank top with a diver flag on it and red shorts yelled over the crowd, interrupting them. "We'll be walking up the dock together, and when we get to the end, you'll need to find the sign for the excursion you have booked. Make sure you know the name of it. We have people there to help you as well."

"Here we go," Brandt said. "Have you ever snorkeled?"

"Yeah."

"Good."

"I promise not to drown you," Summer teased as they walked towards the ship exit.

~

The boat ride to the snorkeling spot was about fifteen minutes, so Brandt and Summer made small talk, mostly about snorkeling. Once they arrived, Brandt shed her clothes down to her swimsuit and began putting on her snorkel vest, mask, and flippers. Her breath caught in her throat when she turned in time to watch Summer pull her tank top over her head and lower her shorts. She was wearing a barely-there bikini that had different shades of purple on the triangle top and bottoms.

"What are you going to do if a fish swims too close and pulls on those strings?" Brandt asked, nodded towards the tiny strings on her hips that where holding her bottoms on.

Summer laughed, "I think I'll be fine." She looked at Brandt standing in front of her and was surprised to see how small her bathing suit was. She wasn't sure what she'd expected, but the flutter in her belly was a surprise. She turned around and got into her gear as the master diver went over the instructions for the reef they were about to snorkel over.

~

After two hours, the air horn blew and everyone began swimming back to the boat. Brandt looked around for Summer, who was about 25 yards away. They met back up on the boat as they removed their gear and stood under the freshwater shower to rinse off.

"Did you see that stingray?" Summer asked. "It must have been three feet wide! I wish I'd had a camera with me."

"Yeah, that's one thing I forgot to pack. I have a few underwater cameras that take great pictures, but I sort of packed in haste. I saw a big turtle and loads of fish."

"Me too," Summer replied, taking her hair down to wring it and shake it out, before wrapping it back up. "I should do that to mine," she said, nodding towards Brandt's short locks, which she simply ran her hands through.

"No. Your hair is gorgeous. Why would you cut it?"

"Because it's a pain in the ass." Summer pulled her shorts and tank top on before sitting down for the boat ride back to the dock. "Do you dye yours that white shade of blonde?"

"No. It's natural. In elementary school the kids used to say I had white hair, not blonde. It used to piss me off. I actually dyed it darker, more like honey blonde in high school, but it looked stupid and I never did it again."

"I think it's cool. It goes with your steel-blue eyes. Which I'm assuming are not contacts either?"

"Nope. My father is purebred Irish on both sides and my mother's family is from Scandinavia and parts of Iceland, mixed with a little English. They are both blonde, but their shades are both darker than mine. I have my mom's same shade of eyes. My dad's are hazel," Brandt answered as she put her shorts and t-shirt back on.

"I have the milkman's eyes," Summer joked. "No one in my family has this shade, but I was told my grandmother had darker green eyes. I never met her. My sister has golden brown colored eyes."

They sat together, watching the shore come back into view a little bit at a time as the boat began the short trip back to the dock.

"This will be the last time I do this for a while," Summer said.

"Why is that? Are you pretty busy with the ship?"

"This is my last cruise. I joined the cast of a reality-style dancing show on TV."

"Wow. That's cool."

"Yeah, it's bittersweet leaving the cruise industry. I've done this for the last five years, cruising every other week to different spots around the world, but my dream is to do bigger and better things."

"What's the name of the show?"

"*Anyone Can Dance*."

"Hmm, I don't think I've heard of it, but I don't watch a lot of TV," Brandt said.

"I don't know much about it. I've seen it a couple of times, but I plan to do a lot of studying when I get off this ship. I've been cast in the show as well as hired as a choreographer for troupe numbers, so this is huge for me."

"It sounds like fun."

"What do you do?" Summer asked.

"I work for a production company called B2 Pictures."

Summer wrinkled her brow. "I don't think I've heard of it."

"We're small and in a niche market."

"What movies have you made? Maybe I've seen them."

Brandt grinned, knowing it was unlikely that Summer had ever seen a movie with lesbians as the main characters, but nevertheless, she named a couple of her award winners. "*That Summer*; *Love Lost and Found*; *Breaking the Rules*. There are about a dozen others. We've been in business for five years."

"*Breaking the Rules* sounds familiar, but I rarely watch TV myself. Every two weeks for the past five years I've been on a cruise ship. I used to work out of Texas, but I changed companies and got moved to California three years ago."

"I guess in the off weeks you don't lose your sea legs. That's probably why you spill coffee on people and rear-end them at red lights," Brandt teased.

Summer playfully smacked her arm. "Yeah, maybe that's it, or I don't know. It could be people walking in through the exit door of the coffee shop or a terrifying bug flying in through my window toward my face!"

Brandt laughed as their boat bumped the dock. Everyone grabbed their belongings and headed back towards the cruise ship.

"There's a huge shopping district right down there," Summer said, pointing to the right.

"Do you want to go?" Brandt asked.

"I've been a few times, but I'll go if you want."

"I promised to bring something back for my friends, so if you don't mind, I'd like to check it out."

Summer checked the time on the small, digital sports watch she was wearing. She needed to be at rehearsal in three hours.

"I have time. Come on, I'll show you the best stores."

The walk was short and Summer grabbed Brandt's hand, pulling her away from the dirty shops. "The ones over here are better," she exclaimed, letting go of her hand.

Brandt simply nodded. She couldn't remember the last time she'd simply held hands with Jenna. She hated thinking of her, but being on their honeymoon made it difficult not to.

"What are you looking for?"

Brandt shrugged. "Something Mexican."

Summer laughed, "Well, that narrows it down."

"They have tequila, sombreros, jewelry, t-shirts, hats—just about anything you can think of."

Brandt looked around in a couple of shops and finally picked out a statue of a drunken, dancing donkey with a little tequila bottle for Viv and a handmade, glass tree ornament for Bean. She also found a t-shirt for herself and Summer bought a couple of things since it was her last trip. Then, they headed back to the ship.

~

After they waited in line to get back on, Brandt checked her watch. The café she'd eaten at the day before was serving lunch and this time it was Asian cuisine.

"Would you like to join me for lunch? I'm only going to the aft deck café, but the food is pretty good," Brandt asked.

"I shouldn't overstay my welcome. We managed to get through the excursion and shopping with no incidents," Summer replied with a smile.

"I wouldn't have asked if I didn't want to," Brandt added.

Summer nodded and followed her to the café. She still had plenty of time and she needed to eat anyway. She was starving from the energy she burned snorkeling around for two hours. She'd never had anything to do with the cruise guests in a social setting, as she usually chose to stay with the entertainment staff who were known to throw some wild parties of their own in the crew area of the ship. But there was something different about Brandt. Maybe it was because they sort of already knew each other. Either way, she liked being around her and didn't want their time together to end. It was nice being in another country and on a ship where no one around them knew her.

She followed Brandt into the line and filled her bowl up with vegetables and pasta, then asked for beef and soy sauce when she handed it to the cook to prepare in the hot wok. Brandt followed suit, choosing beef as well. Then, they found an empty table near a window and sat down to eat.

"Thank you for inviting me today, on the excursion and to lunch. I've had fun," Summer said between bites.

"Thank you for going. It's nice to have someone to talk to that's on the outside. I'm going to have to deal with more than a hundred guests that were anticipating a wedding, including my friends and family. I sort of walked away from everything and boarded the ship the next day," she sighed. "They wouldn't let me cancel it either, so I decided to go and make the best of it."

Summer nodded.

"When I first saw you on that stage, I wanted to jump off and swim back to shore," she smiled and Summer chuckled. "But, I'm glad I've gotten to know you a little bit. You're nothing like the monster I made you out to be."

Summer laughed, "I didn't exactly thing you were the greatest person either."

Brandt held her water glass up. "Here's to a new start and maybe a new friendship."

Summer bumped her glass against Brandt's. "That sounds like a great idea,' she replied before taking a long swallow.

"Honeymoon!" Barney cheered with his glass in the air as he walked by.

Brandt laughed and held her water up to toast with him.

"What the hell?" Summer laughed.

"That's one of the people from my dinner table. They're an interesting group, that's for sure."

"So, they know this is supposed to be your honeymoon?"

"I think the whole boat does, thanks to him," Brandt laughed. "I had to introduce the empty seat next to me after the wait staff announced that I was celebrating my honeymoon. So, I explained my situation and he sort of ran with it. He's nice and it gives me a laugh."

"That's funny." Summer finished water and set the glass down. "I probably need to go get some rest before rehearsal. I had a wonderful time today."

"Me too," Brandt said. "I'm going to try to catch the late show after dinner. I fell asleep last night after spending the day in the sun drinking frozen drinks."

Summer laughed, "Yeah, it'll kick your ass if you're not careful." She stood and moved to hug Brandt like she would any other friend, but changed her mind before it looked too awkward. "Enjoy the rest of your day."

Brandt turned and watched her walk away, wondering how she missed this person during their two altercations. Summer was nothing like Brandt thought she was…nothing at all.

Chapter 11

The captain's dinner was the only formal night for the dining room, so everyone was dressed up for the occasion. The men at Brandt's table were in tuxedos and the women were in cocktail dresses. She'd worn her black tux as well, but opted to go without the vest and tie she'd brought along. Rare cuts of beef and an array of seafood dishes were served and Barney had ordered a couple of bottles of champagne for the table, which Brandt happily helped them drink.

"Any big plans for this evening?" Wilma asked as they finished the last of the bubbly and watched the dining staff clear the table.

"I'm going to the show in the theater, then I was thinking of checking out the night club," Brandt answered.

"We went in there last night, it gets pretty rowdy! We got invited to a private party in the diamond lounge. It's for high rollers in the casino," Wilma replied.

Brandt nodded, thinking it was probably more for heavy losers, but to each his own. "Well, you guys have a wonderful night," she said before leaving their table.

~

Brandt waited outside of the theater for the doors to open and was surprised at the line behind her when everyone was finally allowed inside. She walked down to the front of the stage and took a seat in the second row. A flock of people packed the seats around her in anticipation for one of the entertainment crew's biggest performances. The sign outside had read: '80s Night—Hang On For The Ride!

The distinct strum of a steel guitar brought the sound level of the crowd a few octaves higher as the curtain began to rise above the stage. A few more guitars joined in, followed by a set of drums. Large black speaker boxes that were nearly six feet tall were on both sides of the stage. Brandt heard the roar of a motorcycle as dry ice covered the stage floor in a smoky haze. Then, she watched the shiny chrome and black bike ride out into the center of the stage from the left rear side as Whitesnake's "Still of the Night" blared loudly. One of the male dancers was driving the bike and dressed in jeans, a tight black t-shirt, a leather biker jacket, and boots. The woman on the back with her arms wrapped around him was dressed in a red and black corset, tiny black boy shorts with fishnet stockings, and high heels. She also had on a short-waist style leather biker jacket. Her hair was long and wild with thick waves and curls. Brandt watched as she climbed off the bike in a slow and sexy gesture. Brandt realized it was Summer when she neared one of the spotlights that lit up her face. The guy got off the bike and came up behind her, grinding her from behind as she bent over, swinging her hair around. Then, she stood straight as the music picked up and removed her jacket, tossing it to the back of the stage.

The rest of the cast, who were dressed the same as Summer and the lead guy, ran out as the song quickly changed to another razor-sharp, hair-band song. They quickly paired up in a staggered group to dance a troupe routine of quick and slow, sexy rumba moves mixed with freestyle lifts and spins. The routine followed the music back and forth until it ended. The cast ran off the stage and the men came right back out to do an all-male routine with a concoction of multiple dance styles to Michael Jackson's "Beat It", along with his signature dance from the song, which had the audience clapping along and cheering. Brandt had a huge smile on her face and bobbed her head to the music as she watched the high-energy performance.

The song went right into Michael Jackson's "They Don't Really Care About Us" and the men performed an amazing, completely in-sync step routine to the beat of the music for the first two minutes of the song. Then, the stage went completely black and lit up again with bright spotlights on the female dancers as ZZ Top's "Legs" began playing. Summer was in the middle, leading the women as they danced a short Rockettes-style dance to part of the song while dressed in black corsets with black boy shorts, fish net stockings, and black feather boas around their necks. As the cut of the song ended, it moved right into Madonna's "Express Yourself," which really got the audience going. The dancers moved into a staggered setting and danced a sexy troupe routine that caused them to bend to the floor, swing their hair around a few different times, and shake everything they had to offer.

After the song ended, they ran back stage and Cher's "Turn Back Time" started. The women came back out with the men, pairing up again for the finale, which was another seductive, love/hate style number with a bunch of mixed dance moves from a handful of different dances. The crowd cheered, whistled, and clapped loudly for every twist and turn, aerial lift, hip grind, and near kiss of the dancers.

Brandt held her breath every time Summer was lifted into the air or tossed from one male dancer to another during the entire wild and highly entertaining performance. As soon as the show was over, the dancers came back out as the house lights lit up. The crowd was on their feet as the dancers stood across the stage side by side, waving.

Summer spotted Brandt and smiled brightly. Then, she blew her a quick kiss before running off the stage with the rest of the group.

Brandt was leaning against the stage ten minutes later, when Summer walked out wearing blue warm-up pants and her white Entertainment Crew t-shirt.

"Hey, you," Summer said with a smile, hopping off the stage. "Did you like the show?"

"It was amazing!" Brandt exclaimed. "Did you choreograph any of it?"

Summer grinned. "Most of it."

Brandt nodded. She was impressed with Summer's dancing talent, but she was obviously smart, too, which she also found intriguing. "Do you want to go get a drink with me?"

Summer eyed Brandt's attire. "I'd love to, but I think I'm a little underdressed," she laughed. "Give me a few minutes to go change and I'll meet you somewhere. What bar were you going to?"

"I was going to check out the nightclub, but it doesn't matter to me."

"I'll meet you there in fifteen minutes," Summer stated, hurrying around the side of the stage to head down to the floor that housed the entire crew.

Brandt walked out to the atrium bar and ordered a whiskey, then went down the elevator two decks to the floor where the casino and nightclub were located. She still had ten minutes, so she walked through to see if she saw any of her table mates, whom she found crowded around the craps table.

"Hey!" Betty slurred.

"Honeymoon!" Barney cheered, holding up his glass.

Brandt shook her head and laughed. "I thought you guys were going to a private party."

"Oh, that was over a while ago. Phil's up over a thousand dollars," she giggled.

Brandt looked around, wondering who the hell Phil was, and then it dawned on her that Phil was probably Barney's real name. She smiled and shook her head as she walked the rest of the way through the casino and down the hall towards the nightclub.

Brandt was leaning against the wall outside of the club entrance, sipping the last of her drink when Summer walked up. Brandt almost didn't recognize her in the black, halter-style cocktail dress that was a couple inches above the knee, and high heels, but the beautiful soft brown hair hanging over her left shoulder in spiral waves was unmistakable. The muscles in Brandt's lower belly tightened with a sensation she hadn't felt in a long time.

"Did you start without me?" Summer raised an eyebrow and grinned.

"What? No." Brandt smiled. "I had some time to kill, so I got a drink and walked through the casino. The people from my dinner table are in there losing the farm at the craps table." Brandt set her glass on a nearby table. "You look great. Who knew you cleaned up so well?" Brandt teased. "I actually thought you were a yoga or Pilates instructor from the way you were dressed when you ran into me—twice, I might add."

Summer chuckled, "You ran into me at the coffee shop, but I'll let it slide." She smiled. "Actually, yoga and Pilates are a major part of my exercise routine. They help get me flexible and keep my mind centered. As a dancer, those are two things you have to have. I'm always coming from or heading to an exercise class, the dance studio, or something related, which is why you've only seen me in workout attire."

Brandt nodded. "Well, it's definitely paid off. You're an incredible dancer and an amazing choreographer. I, on the other hand, can't dance worth a shit. I did take some lessons so I could at least dance at my wedding, but that was a waste of money apparently."

"Come on, let's get that drink and you can show me what you learned," Summer said, grabbing her hand and pulling her into the club.

The large room was full of people bobbing and weaving to the beat of the loud music with various dance skills. Summer made her way through the crowd with Brandt in tow.

"Vodka and cranberry; no lime," Summer yelled to the bartender and turned to Brandt.

"Double whiskey on the rocks," Brandt said over the music as she handed the man her room key.

"It's packed in here tonight," Summer stated loudly.

"I wouldn't know. This is my first time in here."

The bartender handed her room key back and slid the drinks across the bar to them. The glasses were smaller than Brandt had expected and looked more like glorious shots than full drinks. Both women moved to the side so other people could order. Summer couldn't help her body wanting to move to the music. Brandt smiled, watching her bob to the beat and was surprised at her own foot tapping along.

Their drinks were finished quickly and Summer grabbed her hand, pulling her out onto the dance floor.

"Let's put those lessons to work!" she exclaimed.

"They were for slower songs!" Brandt laughed as she began moving her hips and arms like most of the crowd. She tried to keep her eyes on Summer's face, away from the cleavage showing and sexy sway of her hips in the form-fitting dress.

Summer grabbed Brandt's hand and spun inside, almost completely against her, before turning back out and twisting to the music. She did this same move four or five times and Brandt simply went with it. She couldn't remember ever having so much fun ever, but especially not in a club.

After a couple more songs, the DJ slowed things down a bit. Brandt gestured for Summer to decided if they stayed on the floor. Summer smiled and stepped into her arms, leaving a lot of space between them as they began to sway to the music. The song had a soft beat similar to a rumba song and Summer couldn't help dancing rumba steps. Brandt caught on quickly, mimicking the movements as best she could. The dance slowly brought them together and by the end, Summer had her arms around Brandt's neck. Brandt's hands were on her lower back and their bodies were pressed together.

When the song ended, Summer pulled away. "Let's go up on the sun deck. I want to get some air and see the stars," she said.

Brandt nodded and followed her out of the club as another thumping song began. There wasn't a cloud in the sky when they reached the top deck and millions of stars were brightly shining around the half moon. They walked over to the railing, looking out at the darkness of the water below.

"I do this a lot after shows—come up here and look at the stars. It's so peaceful and it helps me come down from the adrenaline rush," Summer murmured.

"It's beautiful up here, day or night," Brandt added.

Summer looked up to see Brandt's eyes locked on her. She stared back at the blue eyes and held her breath as butterflies bounced around her stomach. Tearing her eyes away, Summer whispered, "I'm straight. We can be friends, but that's all."

Brandt knew a moment had passed between them. In fact, several moments had passed in the last couple of days, but she wasn't in a place to push the subject anyway. "I'm not looking for a relationship or anything else after what I just went through."

Summer looked longingly into her eyes, then turned away. "I have to go. I'm sorry," she murmured before walking away, leaving Brandt against the railing under the stars.

Brandt let her go. She was slightly confused as to what had just transpired, but either way, she wasn't chasing after anyone...not ever again.

Chapter 12

The next morning, Brandt ate a light breakfast and headed to the couples massage she'd booked months prior and had been unable to cancel along with everything else.

"Ms. Coghlan, welcome to Dream Spa," a cheery woman said. "It looks like you have a couples one-hour massage with us today."

"Yes, but the couple turned into a single at the last minute and apparently your cruise line doesn't allow any cancellations," Brandt sighed.

"Oh, I'm sorry. Since the massage is for two, why don't we break it up into two appointments and schedule you another massage for tomorrow?"

"You can do that?" Brandt asked.

"Sure. You paid for two hour-long massages." The woman smiled.

"That's great!" Brandt exclaimed.

Another woman showed her to the back where Brandt stripped down to a towel and waited in the steam room. Then, she was shown to a small, dimly lit room with a heavily scented floral and eucalyptus aroma. Brandt laid face down on the on the massage table and pulled the towel down to cover her naked butt. The masseuse walked in a minute later and squirted some warm liquid into the palm of her hands.

"I'm going to start with a deep tissue massage to work out any kinks or knots, then I'll move to stone therapy to relax your muscles. After that, you'll move to the steam room to finish the relaxation process."

"Sounds good," Brandt said with her face squished into the open pillow of the table.

~

An hour later, Brandt walked into her room and took a hot shower to wash away the aroma scent from her massage, then she dressed casually in a pair of shorts and a polo shirt with her boat shoes before heading to the art auction. She'd always seen them on cruises but had never actually participated, so she figured, "what the hell, why not?"

As soon as she walked into the room that was the bass-thumping nightclub the previous night, she was handed a glass of champagne. Brandt started at one end and slowly made her way around to all of the paintings, stopping occasionally to look a little closer at pieces she liked.

"Do you see anything you like?" a woman with a heavy French accent asked, sliding up close to her and eyeing Brandt up and down.

Brandt looked at the woman who was wearing a black skirt suit with what looked like no top under the jacket. Her long, dark hair was straight and slicked back and she had big brown eyes. She was pretty and had obviously gone to great lengths to pull off the exotic look.

"I've noticed a couple paintings, but nothing in particular," Brandt answered, sipping her drink.

"Maybe I can help sway your mind," she said, raising an eyebrow. "Show me what you like."

Brandt cleared her throat. She wasn't too familiar with the French, so she wasn't sure if the woman was trying to get her to go to the back room and fuck on top of the paintings, or simply trying to persuade her to buy something.

"I'm going to keep looking. I haven't found anything I can't live without, yet." Brandt finished her champagne and grabbed another glass from a passing waitress.

"You let me know when you do." The woman winked and walked away.

By the time the auction started, she'd drank three glasses of champagne and had two distinct paintings in mind that she wanted for her house. Everyone took their seats in the back of the room for the next two hours as each piece of art was presented and described by the curators and the French woman, who happened to be the art director.

When each of her pieces came up, Brandt waited until there were no more bids before coming in at the last minute to snag each piece. A few people sitting nearby congratulated her and as soon as the auction was over, Brandt rushed to one of the curators to avoid giving her information to the French woman who she was almost certain wanted to do a lot more than just sell her art. Brandt was newly single, and a roll in the sack with a hot foreigner sounded like a good idea, but it wasn't what she wanted or needed. She quickly paid for her two pieces and gave them her office address to have them shipped there instead of her house.

"Congratulations on your new artwork," the French woman said, catching her on the way out.

"Thanks," Brandt replied.

"Maybe I'll see you again before the end of the cruise." She grinned.

"Maybe," Brandt murmured as she walked away towards the elevator. The ice sculpture carving was starting soon on the sun deck and she'd planned to watch it after grabbing a bit to eat for lunch first.

~

When Brandt arrived on the sun deck, a DJ was playing salsa music while the entertainment crew taught dance lessons to the crowd from the small stage. They were dressed in blue shorts, their familiar white t-shirts, and sneakers. She immediately noticed Summer leading the group as they performed the cha-cha. She walked over to the bar and ordered a frozen, fruity drink, then moved back over near the stage to watch her.

The DJ announced the ice carving a few minutes later and the dancers left the stage. Summer locked eyes with Brandt when she walked by and was surprised to see her.

"Hey." Summer smiled, stepping up next to her. "I'm sorry about last night," she sighed.

"It's no big deal. I'm sorry if I made you uncomfortable," Brandt said. She hated walking the fine line with curious straight girls. It wasn't something she cared to do at all, but there was something about Summer that drew her in and a friendship really was all that she was looking for.

"It wasn't that, not at all," Summer replied.

Brandt nodded and left it at that, figuring Summer would say more if she wanted to.

"Are you coming to the show tonight?" Summer asked, locking eyes with her.

"Do you want me to?" Brandt questioned.

"It's Fiesta Night, so it's sexy, salsa style dancing. I think you'll like it. I choreographed a lot of it. Anyway, the late show is much better, so go to that one," Summer stated.

Brandt nodded.

"Enjoy the ice carving. I've seen this at least a hundred times." She started walking away. It's a donkey," she added, over her shoulder with a big smile.

Brandt laughed and shook her head as she watched her go.

~

Summer had been right. After about fifteen minutes, the block of ice had indeed turned into the head of a donkey. Brandt chuckled and headed down to the casino where she found an open slot at the roulette table. She quickly pulled a couple of hundred dollar bills from her pocket.

"Nickels," she said, laying the bills onto the felt.

The dealer handed her a stack of chips similar to the ones she'd had a few days earlier and Brandt went to work playing her favorite numbers straight. When the waitress came around, she shook her head. She'd had enough to drink and would be heading to dinner soon anyway.

A few rolls later, none of Brandt's numbers were hitting and her stack of chips was dangerously low.

"I haven't had the best luck either," an older man next to her said.

"One more roll. All in." Brandt smiled, placing the last stack of six chips straight on the number thirteen.

The man next to her put his last hundred dollars worth of chips on black, the color of the number Brandt bet on. Then, they watched the dealer turn the wheel one direction and spin the white ball in the other. It bounced a couple of times in and out of slots and finally came to a stop on the number thirteen.

"Yes!" Brandt cheered.

"Alright!" the man exclaimed.

"I'm cashing out," Brandt said to the dealer.

"One thousand and fifty dollars coming out," the dealer announced.

Checking her watch, Brandt had just enough time to go get ready for dinner. She rushed back to her room and changed into a dark blue polo shirt and khaki pants. Then, she slipped her boat shoes back on and headed out into the hallway.

"How is your room?" the stewardess asked with a smile when she saw Brandt walk out of her room.

"It's great, Hilda. Thank you," Brandt replied.

"You like your animals?" she said in her thick accent.

Brandt nodded and laughed. She'd been collecting the towel animals each evening and had them lined up on the coffee table in her suite.

"I'll make you a special one tonight." The stewardess smiled. "Maybe two pieces of chocolate." She grinned with a wink.

Brandt nodded and smiled before walking to the stairs.

Chapter 13

Dinner went by quickly since the Flintstones and Rubbles failed to make an appearance. Brandt figured they were probably still in the casino, but she'd hadn't noticed them earlier, so she wasn't sure. As soon as the wait staff cleared the table, she made her way up to the theater where a short line had begun to form.

Once the doors opened, she made her way down to the stage and took a seat in the center of the front row. Slowly, the theater seats filled in around and behind her until there wasn't an open seat available.

"Have you seen any of the shows?" the woman next to her asked.

"Oh, yes. They're very good," Brandt replied.

The woman nodded with a smile as the house lights began to dim.

Brandt's eyes were glued to Summer when she appeared, and remained on her throughout the entire hour-long show. The dance group performed multiple Latin style dances from the salsa to the Paso Doble to an array of different songs, all while wearing various sexy and sometimes barely-there costumes full of bright colors with a lot of sequins.

Watching Summer dance with her bare stomach showing and her hair flying around as her hips swayed and feet moved with the steps of the dances was the sexiest thing Brandt had ever seen. Latin dancing alone already had sex appeal of its own, but Summer had definitely taken it to another level and Brandt loved every minute of it.

At the end of the show, the dance group lined up to bow and Summer smiled, blowing a kiss in Brandt's direction, before heading off the stage. Brandt waited near the stage, and Summer appeared a few minutes later dressed in a tank top and gym shorts.

"Come with me," Summer said, grabbing Brandt's hand and pulling her out of the theater towards the deck exit.

Brandt let herself be led as they moved to the bow of the boat and took the stairs up until they came to a stop on the last deck. Checking to make sure no one was around, Summer stepped up close to Brandt, wrapping her arms around her neck and kissing her like a long lost lover.

Brandt melted into Summer, kissing like her life depended on it. Sliding her arms around Summer, she pulled the shorter woman tightly against her. Brandt couldn't remember ever feeling anything like the sensation of hot blood coursing through her veins, settling low in her belly. She'd never wanted anything or anyone this bad in her entire life, until Summer pulled away from her. Then she'd wanted nothing more than to feel that hunger once again.

"I like you. I can't help being attracted to you," Summer panted.

"I feel it too." Brandt smiled.

Summer shook her head. "This was a bad idea."

A young couple stepped up onto the same deck a few feet away and Summer froze.

"Let's go back to my room," Brandt stated. Seeing the terror in Summer's eyes, she added, "I have a private balcony. We can talk without being bothered. That's all."

Summer blew out the breath she was holding and nodded her head.

Brandt led the way down a couple of decks and towards the staterooms located on the opposite side of the ship. She pulled the key card from her pocket and unlocked the door, holding it open for Summer to enter first.

"This is nice," Summer said, looking around at the spacious suite. "It's better than being cramped four to a room like we are on the crew floor."

"To be honest, it's larger than I expected, or needed, especially being alone, but the private balcony is definitely worth it," Brandt replied.

Summer laughed when she saw the towel animals lined up on the table. The couch across from them hand a big monkey made of towels, and it was stretched out with a mini bottle of rum in one hand and two pieces of candy in the other.

"This is one is neat," Summer said, pointing to the monkey.

"Yeah, that's the one she made tonight. I think my stewardess has a crush on me."

Summer laughed.

"I'm serious," Brandt chuckled, opening the door to the outside deck where a table and two chairs were situated to the right.

Summer walked out to the rail and looked at the vast sea of darkness below with a sky full of stars sparkling above. Brandt stepped up next to her.

"I thought you were straight," Brandt murmured.

Summer turned her head, looking into Brandt's eyes. "It's complicated," she sighed.

"I think I've had enough complication in my life recently. Why don't we just leave it at that," Brandt stated, not really wanting to know about Summer's boyfriends or whatever else the issue was.

"Do you ever wish you could close your eyes and open them somewhere else? Like another life?" Summer whispered.

"I don't know. I guess I used to, but up until recently, I had everything I wanted, or at least, I thought I did," Brandt answered truthfully. "I think the Rolling Stones said it best. You can't always get what you want, but if you try sometimes, you just might find you get what you need."

"And what is it that I need?" Summer asked, looking into her eyes.

"I don't know," Brandt murmured. "You tell me."

Summer closed the gap between them, kissing her passionately. Brandt wrapped her arms around the slightly shorter woman, pulling her close as her hands moved under Summer's tank top to the small of her back. Summer moaned against her mouth and Brandt lost control. She ran her hand lower, cupping Summer's ass and picking her up against her. Summer wrapped her legs around Brandt and kissed her hard.

"Touch me," Summer panted breathlessly in her ear.

Brandt carried her inside and set her down next to the king-sized bed. Clothes were shed as Summer moved back, pulling Brandt down on top of her. They traded soft, teasing kisses as their bodies melded together, skin to skin. Brandt slid down slightly, taking the time to look at the beautiful body under her as she placed delicate kisses over Summer's breasts and taut stomach.

Pale green eyes were staring down, watching her when Brandt looked up as she moved back to her lips. The tender kisses had turned to passionate flames of desire, urging Brandt further with every hitch of Summer's breath. She ran her hand over silky skin to the wetness awaiting her touch. Summer's legs spread instinctively and she moaned loudly as Brandt's fingers circled her throbbing center.

Brandt kissed Summer passionately as her fingers drew circles on her clit, before moving lower, sliding in and out of her. Summer rocked against her, digging her short nails into Brandt's back and biting her lower lip through their fervent kisses.

Feeling Summer's body begin to tighten, Brandt pulled away from her lips and slipped her fingers free as she moved lower, replacing her hand with her mouth, coaxing Summer's body to release with her tongue.

Summer reached down, rubbing her hand over Brandt's cheek as Brandt started to move back up her body. Summer sat up to meeting her halfway with a succulent kiss. Tasting herself on Brandt's lips heightened her senses to another level. They laid together, kissing and cuddling like lovers, until Summer reached her hand down, circling Brandt's clit lazily.

Brandt parted her legs as Summer rolled her to her back and crawled on top of her, careful not to remove her hand as her fingers continued their strokes. Brandt lifting her hips was all the encouragement Summer needed to push her fingers deep inside of her. Brandt kissed her hard and tangled her fingers in Summer's long wavy hair as the climax ripped through her body.

~

Brandt awoke in the middle of the night when she felt the warm body against her stir. She felt surreal when she looked at Summer curled up close to her. The rawness of her body reminded her that it hadn't been a dream. She smiled and brushed the hair from Summer's face. She was just as gorgeous at night as she was during the day. Brandt loved the fact that she barely wore any make-up, except for the show. It made her all the more naturally beautiful. She appeared so young in her sleep, making Brandt wonder how old she really was.

Summer roused and squinted her eyes. Realizing she wasn't in her room and someone was next to her, she pried her eyes opened and looked around until she locked onto the blue ones staring back at her.

"What time is it?" Summer whispered.

"I don't know. The middle of the night probably. I doubt we were asleep for very long."

Summer looked around for a clock. If it was past three a.m.—there was no way she was going to be able to sneak back to her crew room, and everyone would know she'd stayed out all night.

"How old are you?" Brandt asked.

"Huh?" Summer questioned, slightly ignoring her as she continued looking. "Damn it," she huffed, finally seeing the clock by the TV.

"What's wrong?"

"It's too late to go back to my room and everyone's going to know I didn't sleep there."

"Is that a problem?"

"These ships are the biggest gossip chains you'll ever see," she sighed. "At least this is my last cruise and it's over in a day and a half," she added as she lay back on the pillow.

"If you're not working tomorrow during the day, I'd originally planned to rent a vehicle and cruise around Cabo San Lucas."

"What time are you leaving?"

"I guess when we arrive in port."

"There's only a short, twenty minute farewell show since it's the last night, and we're in port, so the entertainment crew is actually off for the day. We have to prepare for disembarkation the following morning and be up extremely early. I definitely won't be out late." Summer leaned over, smiling at Brandt before kissing her lips softly. "I guess I'll meet you on the dock when we arrive," she murmured, curling up against her.

Chapter 14

The next afternoon, Brandt stepped off the ship, stretching like a Cheshire cat in the warm sun. Summer laughed as she leaned against the rail, watching her.

"Hey," Brandt said, walking up to her. "You were gone when I woke up."

"I needed to take a shower and eat breakfast," she replied, falling in step with her. "I'm glad I decided to join you today."

"Did your roommates wonder where you were last night?"

Summer nodded. "So, what's on the agenda?"

"I figured we'd drive around in my rental, maybe bar hop along the coast and take in the local scene," Brandt answered.

"Sounds like fun." Summer smiled.

Brandt checked her rental information so she went to the correct location since there were a few different rental shops near the cruise port. Finding the correct one, she walked with her ID and credit card in hand. The man behind the counter spoke broken English as he explained the contract. Understanding him, she nodded and signed where he pointed, then walked outside with Summer to wait for their car to be brought around.

"Here's your rental," Summer laughed, pointing to the ragged-out Jeep with the top off coming down the road.

"Yeah, right," Brandt chuckled.

The orange vehicle rolled to a stop in front of them and the driver held his hand out to her when he opened the door.

"You've got to be kidding me," Brandt huffed. "Tell me this isn't what I rented."

The man looked at the papers and smiled at her. Then, he checked the gas gauge and circled the corresponding amount on the paperwork.

"Have it back by three o'clock," he said in broken English, handing her the paperwork and walking away.

Brandt's jaw was wide open in shock.

"Come on," Summer laughed as she walked around to the passenger side.

"It's a piece of shit!" Brandt shook her head.

"Are you up for a little adventure?"

"Yeah, but I don't want to get stranded on the side of the road in a foreign country where they don't speak English!"

"Either you get in or I'm driving and you can ride in the back," Summer stated. "You rented it. It's a done deal. Let's go!"

Brandt climbed in, cursing when she had to slam the door hard to get it closed. She quickly pulled on her seatbelt and pushed the clutch in, feeling it engage just before it hit the floorboard. The gearshift knob had been replaced with a golf ball, so she had to guess the gear pattern and figured it was a six-speed like her car. She put it in first and bounced down the road on the bald tires and worn suspension while Summer chuckled.

"I need a drink!" Brandt laughed hysterically. "I can't believe this is my luxury rental car!"

Summer looked at the local map the man gave them. "I think there's a bar about a mile up ahead."

All of the signs were in Spanish and although she didn't speak it, Brandt knew enough of the language to get by. She worked her way through the gears as they left the tourist area and headed up the coast. The only thing separating the road they were on and the waves of the Pacific Ocean was tan colored sand and large rocks in some areas. They drove away from the tourist area of Playa del Amor and found an open stretch of coastal road.

"This is awesome!" Summer yelled as she held her hands up in the wind.

Brandt smiled. There was no way Jenna would've gotten into the raggedy vehicle and called it an adventure. Looking at the woman next to her, Brandt shook her head. She still couldn't believe running into Summer on the ship. She was sure the trip was doomed and would be full of bad luck since that seemed to be all that surrounded them when they were in the same vicinity. Her mind drifted back to the night before. The last thing Brandt ever thought she'd be doing on her honeymoon was having sex with someone she barely knew, and especially not to mention her nemesis, but Bean would tell her it happened for a reason. Maybe one day she'd know what that reason was. Either way, she was having fun and it felt great.

Brandt slowed, seeing a small building on the side of the road that looked like a tiki hut. She pulled off into the sand and cut the engine. "I think we're here," she said, stepping out of the vehicle.

"This is a bar?" Summer questioned, following her.

There were no walls, only posts holding up the tiki-style roof over the large bar with stools all around. It looked like something you'd find at a resort by the pool, except it was on the side of road and definitely had its share of patrons. Nearly 100 t-shirts were attached up under the roof. Most had names and dates written on them, and Latin music was blasting from a radio somewhere behind the bar. Brandt looked at Summer and smiled as they sat on a rickety pair of stools.

"Hola! Quieres beber?" a man with a thick Spanish accent popped his head up from where he'd been bending down a few feet away, stocking the bar.

"What are you drinking?" Brandt asked Summer.

"Nothing with water in it. You'll get the shits for a week."

"Yeah, I know," Brandt laughed. "Do you drink beer?"

"It's not my favorite thing in the world, but that's fine."

"Cerveza," Brandt said, holding two fingers up.

The man nodded, pulling two bottles of beer from the cooler he'd been stocking. He used a rusty bottle opener to pop the tops and slid the ice-cold beverages over to them. Brandt smiled and wiped the top with the tail of her shirt before taking a long sip.

"This is nice," Summer murmured, looking out at the waves lapping the shore 30 feet away.

"Yeah," Brandt whispered.

"Do you see all of those shirts? How cool is that? It looks like people have written on their shirts and left them behind for the ceiling."

"It's definitely different," Brandt agreed.

"I'm going to do it," Summer replied as she pulled her tank top off, revealing her sports bra.

Brandt's jaw nearly hit the counter. "Don't you need a shirt?"

Summer smiled. "I'm wearing a sports bra, silly. It covers more than my bathing suit. Come on, it's your honeymoon, live a little," she teased. "I did see a little case with stuff in it over there when we walked up. Maybe they sell shirts with the bar's name on them," she added.

Brandt laughed.

The bartender handed her a sharpie marker when he saw her shirt lying in front of her.

"What should we write on here?" Summer asked.

"We? It's your shirt."

"You're with me." Summer smiled. "I wouldn't be here if it wasn't for you. Oh, I have a great idea."

Summer took the marker and wrote the word "HONEYMOON" across the front of the tank top with a huge X through it. Then, she wrote her and Brandt's names and the date. "What do you think?" she asked, holding it up.

Brandt shook her head and laughed. "I like it." There was something about this carefree, contagiously happy woman

Summer gave it to the man, who immediately put it up on the wall with the others. Then, he returned with a box of shirts they had for sale. Summer searched until she found a small, hot pink tank top with an outline of the tiki bar in blue and the name of the bar written under it, also in blue.

"He probably thinks we're on our honeymoon," Brandt laughed.

"I didn't think of that," Summer chuckled. "Oh, well." She shrugged, still smiling.

By the time they started their second beer, a few other vehicles had stopped at the roadside bar. Brandt figured they were rentals too from their state of distress. She and Summer nodded and smiled as the other couples sat around the bar.

"So, tell me more about this show you're doing," Brandt said.

"It has a group of pro dancers such as myself, and they bring average people onto the show and pair them with us for ten weeks. Each week we have a new dance, which we choreograph for our partner, and then we dance it for the audience on live TV. There are no judges, only the people who watch and vote for their favorite. We get constructive criticism from retired pros who sit on the sidelines, so that sometimes sways the vote a little bit. Each pair does the same style of dance, but we get to pick our music and costumes and choreograph it our way, so every pair is a little different. There are also troupe numbers where all of the pros dance together."

"That's interesting. So, do the average partners get kicked off like in a regular reality show?"

"No. Everyone stays until the end. The votes are tallied each week and you're scored based on the amount of votes you receive. That's the order in which you dance the next week, with the lowest score going first and so on. There are only six pros and only the top three get to compete in the finale, which takes votes during the entire show and reveals the winner in the end. You do three dances of your choice for that show."

"I'll have to check into getting tickets," Brandt replied.

Summer motioned to the guy behind the bar for paper and a pen. He returned with their bill, which made Brandt laugh hysterically. Summer wrote down her cell number on a blank section of the bill and tore it off, handing it to Brandt. Then, Brandt did the same and slid the paper into her pocket before tossing enough pesos on top of the bill to leave a hefty tip. The bartender smiled and waved.

"Where do you want to go next?" Brandt asked when she climbed into their raggedy rental. "All of the cars around here are worn out pieces of shit."

Summer chucked. "Let's find some live music," she said.

"Sounds good." Brandt turned the key and the motor spit, sputtered, shook, and puffed smoke before finally starting.

Summer laughed hysterically and waved at the bar as Brandt drove away in embarrassment. They continued a few more miles down the road and came to a stop at another beach establishment with a pile of shitty rental vehicles scattered around on the sides of the road. Summer's hips moved subconsciously to the beat of the Latin music the band was playing. The few people on the dance floor and scattered around the bar were tourists from the cruise ships and nearby resorts. Summer pointed at the tequila and held up two fingers when she and Brandt walked up to the bar. The Spanish man smiled and retrieved the shot glasses, pouring each one to the top. She shook her head when he offered lime and salt.

"Happy honeymoon!" Summer cheered, clinking her glass to Brandt's and chugging it down.

Brandt laughed and swallowed the bitter shot. Summer wiggled her brows and smiled brightly as she grabbed Brandt's hands, pulling her into the dance floor. Brandt followed and quickly picked up the steps as Summer danced the Merengue in front of her.

When the song ended, they had another set of shots and moved right back to the dance floor. Brandt had no idea what she was doing, simply following along with Summer's hips and feet, but it felt great. They moved to a closed position, dancing together and making the rest of the people on the makeshift dance floor look like they had two left feet. Brandt held Summer's hand over her head and smiled as she turned.

After nearly a dozen songs, Brandt and Summer finally walked off the dance floor and walked through the hot sand towards the water. The sunscreen Brandt had put on earlier that day was starting to wear off and the scorching rays of the sun were started to turn her skin pink.

"It's a hell of a lot hotter here than L.A.," Summer said.

"No kidding. I don't know how they live here."

"This is why," Summer replied, holding her arms out. "It's like living in paradise."

"Yeah, but this isn't how they live. This is how the tourists see Mexico. If you turn off some of the side roads we passed, you'll see the huts and shacks they really live in. I saw it when I was in Cozumel a couple of years ago on vacation. The people that live in that island don't live in the best conditions, but the tourist area is beautiful," Brandt stated, walking away from the noise of the bar.

"I've been on different ships and seen a lot of different countries. They always make me glad to do what I do and live where I live. Clean running water and a toilet are luxuries to some people," Summer said, walking next to her.

"Am I going to see you when we get home?" Brandt asked, tossing a small rock into the waves.

"Do you want to see me?"

Brandt looked at her, wishing she could see the beautiful eyes behind the dark sunglasses. "If you'd asked me that when I saw you on the first day of the cruise, I would've probably told you I'd rather chew my own leg off than see you again." She grinned. "I've really enjoyed spending time with you, Summer. I'm not looking for a relationship, but I definitely want to see you again. I have a lot to deal with when I get back, which is probably an understatement."

"Yeah, I have a lot going on with the show, but I'd like to see you too. I've had more fun in the last few days than I can remember," Summer replied, linking her hand with Brandt's as they walked.

Brandt stopped near a large rock next to the water. "Getting to know you and spending time with you has been the best part of this trip," she said, pulling Summer into her arms, kissing her passionately as the heat of the scorching afternoon sun shined through her clothing, burning her skin. Summer pulled away, placing another quick kiss on Brandt's lips, before checking the watch on her wrist.

"Do you need to get back?" Brandt asked.

"Yeah. I wish I didn't," Summer murmured.

Brandt pulled her close and held her tightly one more time before walking back to the Jeep. They both climbed in, buckling the stretched out seatbelts that didn't tighten.

"What's the point of wearing these?" Summer asked.

"Who knows," Brandt said, pushing the clutch in and turning the key. The motor coughed and sputtered before shutting off. Brandt turned it again with the same results. "Come on you piece of shit," she growled, turning it again.

When the engine tried to catch, she pressed the gas pedal to breathe a little life into the motor. It sound like it was going to cut off again, so she floored the gas a few times, revving it loudly. Summer shook her head, laughing as Brandt put it in gear and drove away, peeling out slightly in the loose sand on the asphalt.

~

Back on the ship, Summer gave her a quick hug and told her she'd see her up on the sun deck after the last performance, before heading off to rehearse for the show and get ready for disembarkation. Brandt went to her much needed spa appointment and then dinner, where her table mates surprised her with a bottle of champagne to celebrate her honeymoon week. She sat around with them after dinner until the show was about to start, then went to go watch the finale.

The final show was all about the cruise line and very cheesy. It reminded her of the show *The Love Boat*, and maybe that's exactly what the cruise director was going for since he was the center of attention for the show. After it was over, Brandt headed up to the sun deck and sat in one of the lounge chairs near the stern where she looked up at the stars and listened to the lull of the props moving the ship through the water.

~

Two hours later, a pair of stumbling cruise guests made some noise on the other side of the deck, waking Brandt from the sleep she'd fallen into. Checking her watch, she knew Summer should've already shown up, so she headed back to her room to pack and get ready to face reality. She hated not saying goodbye to Summer, but they'd exchanged numbers and made plans to get together. She thought of going to look for her, but figured the young woman was caught up in her last night as a cruise line employee.

As soon as she'd finished packing, Brandt took some pictures of her towel animals to show Bean and crawled into the bed. She didn't open her eyes again until they were back in the port in Long Beach, California.

Chapter 15

Brandt went through the three-hour disembarkation process the next morning without seeing Summer again. She knew the crew was very busy the last night of the cruise, so she figured that's what had kept Summer away. Brandt hadn't gone on her honeymoon to meet anyone, but she'd wound having a much better time than expected and wasn't ready to be home.

When she walked through the terminal with her suitcase, Brandt's joyous attitude changed, remembering her car was in the shop and the reason why. She headed over to the taxi lane and hopped into a cab, reciting her address. The driver turned the meter on and drove off before she could change her mind, not that she would or could anyway, but the fare was going to be hefty for the thirty-mile trip. Brandt could've called Bean to come get her, but she wasn't ready for that conversation. She knew she'd have a ton of things to do when she arrived at home, but for the next forty-five minutes, she wanted to remain free of constraints of her own life and enjoy the last little bit of her vacation.

Brandt cursed the 405 for being free of traffic, allowing the driver to get her home quicker than she'd anticipated. She input the code when he pulled up at her gate. The wrought iron bars spread apart and he pulled through the circular drive near the front door. She handed him one hundred and twenty dollars cash, enough to cover her fare and leave him with a generous tip, before getting out.

~

Brandt's cell phone had over one hundred emails, close to seventy text messages from forty different people, and nearly fifty voicemails when she picked it up off the counter and turned it on.

"Holy shit," she exclaimed, shaking her head as she scrolled through the list. Not one single missed call, text message, or email was from Jenna. It wasn't like she expected it, but after three years, she'd hoped they cared a little more for each than a handwritten couple of lines to say it's over. Brandt deleted all of the messages without listening to or reading any of them, and headed upstairs to unpack her bag before taking a long hot shower.

She finally emerged from her bedroom clean and refreshed and walked into her home office where she sat down behind her desk, scrolling through the contacts on her phone for the one person she'd needed to talk to the most.

"Welcome back," Bean said.

Brandt knew she wasn't talking about the cruise. No, Bean was more literal than that and had been referring to the abrupt hiatus Brandt had taken by completely shutting everyone out.

"Hey," Brandt sighed.

"I'm here for you, whatever you want. If you feel like crying, I have two shoulders. If you want to smash some shit, I'll buy a bat. Whatever you need me to do."

Brandt laughed. "Can you find Jenna and put a horse's head in her bed? Or better yet, bring me her head?"

"Well," Bean paused. "I don't know any mobsters, but I can make it happen."

"Knowing you, I believe you," Brandt chuckled, then sighed. "Actually, some company would be nice and maybe a bottle of wine."

"See you in a bit," Bean replied as she hung up.

Brandt called her parents and gave them a roundabout explanation for what had happened and hung up quickly with a promise to see them soon. She thought about sitting on the pool deck, her favorite place, but the warm sun reminded her of the cruise and she simply wasn't ready to go there yet. She was still trying to wrap her head around everything that had transpired during the seven-day trip.

When Bean arrived, Brandt was lounging on the couch with her feet on the coffee table, scrolling through the channels on the TV. She moved to answer the door but heard the lock click, meaning Bean had used her key, so she settled back down.

Bean walked into the dining room, grabbing two glasses and the wine opener from the china cabinet, before sitting down next to Brandt on the couch.

"Only you," Brandt laughed.

Bean shrugged and opened the bottle of wine, pouring a generous amount into both glasses. She handed one to her best friend as she sat back and said, "Start at the beginning and leave nothing out."

"Hell," Brandt huffed, taking a sip of the merlot. "I don't even know where that is anymore. Do I start at the beginning of the three-year relationship that was

111

apparently a lot less than I thought it was? Or do I skip to the honeymoon I took alone?"

"I'm sorry." Bean shook her head and squeezed her best friend's hand. "What a cluster fuck."

"No kidding, and it just keeps building!" Brandt exclaimed.

"What do you mean? Did Jenna contact you?"

"No. That's long over. She ran off with the fucking wedding planner of all people," Brandt sneered.

"That no-good bitch didn't deserve you to begin with."

"Where the hell did it all go wrong, Bean? Was I blindly living a lie? I just...I don't get it."

"I don't know, hon."

"I've thought about it more than I cared to and I honestly think we grew worlds apart in this last year. I can't fault her if she wasn't happy, but why go through with the wedding in the first place? That's what has me so pissed off. She could've called it off and ended things months ago!"

"You know everything with Jenna was a show. She was all about impressing people."

"Well, she planned the biggest show of her life, the fucking masterpiece, and didn't even make an appearance. She left that letter for me and hopped on the first plane to New York. So, why do it?"

Bean shook her head and pushed her black framed glasses back up on her nose as sipped her wine. "I've never been in either or your positions, so I can't really say. It makes no sense when you put it that way, though. Why plan it if you're not going to be there anyway?"

"Exactly my point. I'm not even sad that it's over. If she wants to be with someone else or find herself or whatever the fuck she's calling it, then fine. I won't say it didn't hurt. I was crushed when I read that letter, but I'm not going to waste my life and my time on someone who doesn't want to be with me. Not to mention, someone without a stitch of class, or respect for me and my family." Brandt finished her wine and poured another glass.

"Yeah, the way she did things was beyond shitty. She's obviously a selfish, first-class asshole."

"Good riddance! I'm better off without that bitch!" Brandt cheered.

"I'll drink to that!" Bean exclaimed.

"I think I'm more pissed at myself for not seeing it coming. I let her blindside me."

Bean nodded. "I'd like to strangle her, but then I'd be making prison movies."

Brandt laughed. "Oh, I thought of the same damn thing."

"How was the cruise? You know I would've went with you, so you didn't have to go by yourself."

Brandt smiled. "I know and I love you for that, but I had to do it alone. You'd be surprised at how quickly you get over someone who fucks you over and leaves you at the altar."

"I wouldn't know, but I think I'd be more pissed than sad."

"Exactly!"

"So, did you meet anyone? The best way to get over a woman is to get under a different one, which I'm hoping you did." Bean wiggled her eyebrows.

Brandt laughed. "You'll never believe who I ran into."

"If it was Jenna or the wedding planner, I hope you pushed them overboard."

Brandt shook her head. "Worse than that almost."

"Huh?"

"Who is the last person I wanted near me, besides Jenna, of course?"

Bean pursed her lips and scrunched her brow, making her resemble a mouse. "I don't know." She shrugged.

"Where's my car?"

"The garage…oh…" Bean's eyes grew as round as saucers behind her lenses. "No! The hot yoga chick who keeps running into you? She was on the cruise?"

Brandt nodded.

"Oh, my God! How did you make it home alive?"

Brandt laughed, "It wasn't easy." She sipped her wine. "In fact, she works on the ship, or did. Anyway, she was part of the entertainment crew that did nightly shows. She's a dancer and choreographer, not a yoga instructor, by the way."

"Did she do something to you?"

Brandt grinned, thinking about the time they shared together. "I saw her on the first day when we had to muster and thought I was going to drown for sure, and I was on the cruise from hell, but she turned out to be a lot of fun. I took her snorkeling with me and—"

"What?" Bean said, cutting her off. "You actually hung out with her?"

"She's a really interesting person and extremely talented. I've never seen anyone dance the way she does. It's mesmerizing."

114

"It sounds like something, alright," Bean stated, shaking her head. "Are you sure you didn't bang your head in that accident?"

Brandt laughed. "I really enjoyed spending time with her and I plan to see her again soon. Have you ever heard of a reality dancing show with average people as contestants?"

"I saw a commercial about something like that. Why?"

"She was just cast as one of their pro dancers and choreographers. That cruise was her last one…you know how you're always saying everything happens for a reason?" Brandt shrugged.

"Yeah and sometimes the reasons aren't that great. Don't you think you need some time for the dust to settle before you get back on the horse and ride off into the sunset with the person who is a magnet for disaster?" Bean wondered.

"We made plans to see each other again, but there are no strings and I'm definitely not looking to get into a serious relationship again anytime soon. We had a lot of fun together and…I like her, Bean. She's genuine and it's been a long time since I was around someone like that, but I'm not chasing after anyone. Jenna led me around like a dog on a leash and I'm never doing that again."

"I don't blame you. After what you went through, you deserve a hell of a lot better the next time around, no matter who she is, but the single life isn't so bad once you give it a try."

"Bean, you're only single because you chose to be."

"Exactly, it's my choice."

Brandt smiled and shook her head.

"So, this mysterious dancer, what's her name?"

"Oh, yeah, sorry. Her name's Summer."

"Last name?"

"I forgot. Why, are you going to Google her?" Brandt chuckled.

"You can't be too careful. This entire thing could be an elaborate setup. First the coffee, then the accident, and now, the cruise. Maybe it was a ploy of some kind."

Brandt laughed, "I thought I was the writer."

"Oh, I'm seeing this as a movie playing out right in front of me. Lunatic woman escapes the nuthouse and goes after Hollywood's most eligible lesbian, taking her for everything she has and leaving her for dead."

"Oh, nice!" Brandt chided.

"I'm kidding. I'm glad you found a way to turn a shitty situation into a good time and had fun, no matter who it was with," Bean said, pouring the last of the bottle into their glasses.

"I have so much crap to do this week. The bitch stuck me with the wedding bill, so I need to make sure everything was finalized, and I need to get those gifts on the dining table sent back."

"I think you should sue her. She's the one who dumped you at the altar with a damn note of all things."

Brandt shrugged. "I'd love to stick it to her, but honestly, I'm over the whole damn thing. I just want to move on with my life and put her and these last three years behind me."

"I better never see her in L.A. again. You'll be bailing me out of jail," Bean growled.

"You mentioned breaking shit—I have an idea." Brandt ran upstairs and returned with an 8x10" picture and the pistol she kept in her nightstand in case of a home

116

invasion. She set the gun on the table and grabbed the two large pictures hanging on the wall behind the bar. "I bought replacements for these, so let's go break shit."

Bean nodded and followed her outside. Brandt's house was on the side of the maintain overlooking a valley with a picturesque view of the next mountain in the distance.

"Toss the picture over the rail and high into the air," Brandt said, making a Frisbee-style motion.

"What are you going to do?" Bean asked.

Brandt grinned and nodded for her to toss the picture. Bean sighed and tossed up as high as she could out over the rail. Brandt held her pistol out and squeezed the trigger. BANG! The gun went off and the picture shattered to pieces.

Bean laughed hysterically. "Oh, my God, that's crazy!"

"Feels great!"

"Wouldn't it be better to just use a baseball bat?"

"No. I'd get glass on the deck and in the pool. This way's better. Do it again!" Brandt steadied her gun and pulled the trigger as soon as the picture was high in the air. "Woo hoo!" she cheered.

Bean tossed up the last framed photo and Brandt quickly shot it. Then, they rushed into the house where she put the gun away.

"What if your neighbors call the cops?" Bean asked, watching her walk back down the stairs.

Brandt shrugged. "Either way, it felt great."

"Who are you? And what have you done with my easy-going, laidback, best friend?" Bean laughed.

Brandt chuckled. "Come on, help me get these gifts re-addressed so I can send them out Monday."

Chapter 16

In the middle of the following week, Brandt had called Summer and left a voicemail asking her to lunch, but she never heard back from her. Figuring it was probably for the best, she didn't bother contacting her again and deleted the number from her phone.

A week later, she and Bean flew up to Vancouver to find a location for their next movie and to meet with the set design team and film crew. Their newest picture was a thrilling love story about two women who were madly in love with each other, despite being married to other people. They sneak off to a bed and breakfast every chance they get. After a few months, the wives find out and make a pact to kill them both, making it look like a twisted murder suicide.

It was a story Brandt had written, so she was very involved with the process from the casting of the actors to choosing the shooting location. She was 100 percent dedicated to every movie the company made since she was a producer, but she threw herself further into the project when it was her personal script. Brandt welcomed the busy, long hours that helped keep her mind on track and focused.

After riding up and down the coast, Brandt and Bean came back to the first B&B they'd stopped at.

"I think this one will work," Bean said, turning into the parking lot.

"I liked the one that was closer to the water," Brandt stated.

"Me too, but this one has everything we are looking for and it's cheaper since it's not corporately owned. We'll be able to fit it into our budget."

"I know," Brandt replied, getting out. "I love the way the air smells up here. It is so crisp and clean."

"That's because they don't have smog," Bean laughed.

Brandt followed her inside, helping to negotiate a deal to rent the entire place out for the next month as well as making a few necessary changes to accommodate their set design. After the hour-long meeting, Bean called the office and had Renee fax the contract to the owner's of the B&B while Brandt drove them to the meeting with the design team and film crew at the hotel at which they were staying.

Bean went over the basic info with the film guys while Brandt laid out the set with the design manager. He had one week to have the set built for the only room they'd be filming in, but they'd also planned to turn the dining area into a makeshift living room for one of the women's houses and use the actual B&B living room for the other, with a few adjustments, of course. The film crew was scheduled to arrive in one week to start blocking and get set up, then the cast would arrive two days after that for twenty straight days of shooting.

After the meetings, Brandt and Bean headed to the airport to catch their flight home.

"I'm looking forward to this film. I like them all and I never try to single any of my scripts out, but the timing for this one couldn't be better," Brandt said.

"I agree," Bean replied.

~

The next two weeks went by in a blur. Bean and Brandt were rushing around trying to finalize everything for the new movie, from the costume design to the set colors and actors hairstyles. The design crew was already building part of the set at an offsite location so that all they had to do was put it together once they were on location in a week. Brandt's birthday had also come and gone. She hadn't wanted to do much, so Bean came over with a bottle of wine and they drank the night away.

"Hey, have you heard from that cruise ship dancer...what was her name? Summer?" Bean asked. They were sitting in a Japanese restaurant having sushi for lunch.

Brandt had tried not to think about Summer, but when she closed her eyes, she often saw her in her bed, naked and wanting. She found herself scanning the crowds of people in stores and on sidewalks looking for her beautiful smile, until she finally gave up on seeing her again altogether and threw herself headlong into the new film.

"No. It wasn't meant to be, I guess," Brandt said. "It's not like I was looking for a relationship anyway."

Bean heard the sorrow in her voice and wondered just how close they'd actually got during that trip. She'd noticed Brandt was hovering more than usual with the new movie and had a feeling she was trying to keep her mind busy. She wasn't sure what to say. In the past month, her best friend had been through hell and back, and Summer had played a large role with one disaster after another.

"Do you think it would be odd to bring a date to the screening this weekend?" Bean asked, changing the subject. Brandt's film that Viv had been busy editing, was finally completed and ready for screening at the local film festival, which Bean and Brandt had planned to attend along with the two main actors.

Brandt raised an eyebrow and stopped her chopsticks mid-bite.

"What?" Bean huffed. "I go on dates."

"Since when?"

"I don't know. It's nothing, really. I met someone and I was thinking of taking her. Do you think that's weird?"

"Who is this someone?" Brandt asked.

Bean looked around the room and whispered, "She's Viv's cousin."

Brandt thought for a minute. "Misty? Hasn't she worked on a few of our films?"

"Yeah. She's a make-up artist."

Brandt tried to remember what the woman looked like, but only remembered her being eccentric and quite the opposite of Bean's nerdy personality. "I think you should do whatever makes you happy," Brandt said.

"I didn't imply she and I were an item," Bean laughed. "I know she's done a lot of work for us and I was thinking about asking her to go with me. I think she'd like it."

"Well, then ask her."

"Fine," Bean said, pulling her phone from her pocket and scrolling through her contacts.

"I didn't mean this second," Brandt murmured as Bean ignored her and talked to the woman on the other end of the line.

"She has plans," Bean stated hanging up.

"Shit happens," Brandt replied.

"But, she's changing them to go with me." Bean smiled.

Brandt laughed.

Chapter 17

The screening had gone well over the weekend, giving Brandt and Bean a boost of confidence as they prepared to film their next picture. All of their movies went directly to DVD and were distributed worldwide through various marketers. Then, after a year on DVD, they were released on Netflix and sometimes shown on LGBT television stations around the world. Brandt and Bean were hoping to produce a movie one day that would take the film festivals by storm and be released on the big screen as a feature film.

They had less than a week to go before they needed to be in Vancouver for the final prep of the set and to start shooting the film. Since Bean was the director, she had gone up a couple of days early to make sure everything was on schedule.

It was quiet in the office without Bean talking her ears off, so Brandt decided to change the atmosphere around her. "I'm going to lunch. Send my calls to my voicemail," she said to Renee before walking out the front door of the building.

Brandt slid into the contoured leather seat of her car and sped down the road a couple of blocks to a popular soup, salad, and sandwich place that Bean always boasted about. She parked in the back lot and walked around to the front door. She froze when she took in the woman walking towards her, seemingly going into the same restaurant.

"I'd say fancy meeting you here, but I'd be lying," she said.

"I'm sorry I didn't return your call," Summer sighed. "Things have been crazy with the show about to start."

Brandt eyed her up and down. Summer looked as good as ever, dressed in baggy warm-up pants, sneakers, and sports bra with a short-waist style hoodie over it. Her hair was up in a ponytail with curly tendrils hanging down, and she had dark sunglasses covering her pretty, light green eyes.

"Are you going in?" Brandt questioned.

Summer nodded.

"Would you like to join me?"

Summer looked around first, then replied, "Sure."

They walked inside together and were shown to a booth in the back.

"What happened the last night of the cruise?" Brandt asked.

"I'm sorry. The entertainment crew threw me a goodbye party and the next morning, I was assigned to baggage."

Brandt couldn't really say anything negative. She wasn't looking for a relationship and if whatever it was they shared on the cruise was just that, a few shared moments, then she understood why Summer had avoided her.

"I understand," Brandt said, pausing to order a glass of water and a salad from the waitress. "You must live nearby. I always seem to run into you in this area," she continued, changing the subject.

Summer smiled. "The dance studio I rehearse at is a couple blocks away."

"I see. So, how are things going with the show?"

"Hectic to say the least. The season is ten weeks long, then it's off for four months. After that, it runs again for another ten-week season. I get comp tickets for friends and family, so I'll definitely send you some. If you want to go, that is."

"I'd love to. Thank you for thinking of me."

"Will you be bringing anyone?" Summer asked casually.

Brandt gave her a questioning look.

"I need to know how many tickets to send you," Summer added.

Brandt nodded. "I don't know. It'll probably just be me, but I may bring a friend."

Summer bit her bottom lip. "I'll send you a pair then." She smiled as the waitress set their lunch plates on the table and walked away once again.

"What do you plan to do for the four month off-season between shows?"

"I don't know. I might go back on the cruise ship for a little bit, but once the show has started, people will recognize me more. Plus, I can't really do both and you have to commit for a minimum of six months with the cruise line."

"That makes sense. Are you choreographing on the show too?"

"Yes, a little here and there to start, but that's part of the reason I was hired. There's a lot that goes into the show, especially with all of the single numbers, and the troupe choreography alone takes a few days to put together and another few days or more to learn."

"Wow. I didn't realize it was so intricate."

"We also have a lot of appearances to make before the start of the season and of course after it ends. My off time will be limited to probably two months, maybe less, but I was actually thinking of working with movies one day, so I may try my hand at that in the off season as well. At least a little at a time."

"It sounds like you know what you're doing."

Summer smiled. "It's more like controlled chaos."

Brandt laughed.

"What about you? What have you been doing since you got back?" Summer asked.

"Oh, a little of this and a little of that," Brandt shrugged, pushing her empty salad plate aside. Realizing Summer was waiting for more, she continued. "I spent the first week putting my non-existent wedding behind me—making calls, sending back gifts, and so on. I've also been doing a lot of traveling for work lately."

"It sounds like you've been pretty busy yourself."

"Yeah, just a little bit." Brandt grinned, slipping her card into the folder for her bill. "Hey, would you like to come over for dinner, maybe tomorrow night?"

"At your house?" Summer asked, biting her lower lip as she placed some cash into her bill folder.

"Yeah. Do you like steak?" Brandt asked.

Summer shrugged. "I don't eat a lot of red meat, but..." She thought for a second.

"I don't either, but I haven't had it since the cruise, so I was thinking of cooking on the grill."

"Okay, sure. Can I bring anything?"

"No. I have it covered. I'll see you tomorrow around, say, six?" Brandt signed her credit card slip. She then wrote her phone number and address on the back of her receipt, along with the code to her gate, and slid it across the table to Summer.

"That's fine." Summer glanced at the paper. "You live in Santa Monica?"

"Yes."

"I guess I figured you lived around here."

"My office is nearby. Have you ever been to Santa Monica?"

Summer shook her head.

"It's easy. You can take Santa Monica Boulevard all the way, then there are a few side streets you have to take to get to my house once you get into town."

"Alright. I guess I'll see you tomorrow night." Summer smiled.

Brandt stood and walked with her. They went their separate ways outside of the door since Summer was parking in the front and Brandt's car was in the back. Brandt took a minute to call Bean and see how things were going before heading back to the office. She was scheduled to fly up on Sunday to join everyone and Bean reassured her that everything was going fine. She said they were actually a day ahead of schedule, so they were taking the extra time to go over last minute adjustments to make sure every scene was perfect so they didn't have to do multiple takes. That's part of the reason micro-budget and low-budget films were successful with staying on budget—they couldn't afford more than two or three takes at the most of each scene.

Chapter 18

Brandt spent the next day rushing around the office trying to finish up some last minute paperwork and finalize the release of her latest movie that had just finished screening. Then, she headed home, stopping at the grocery store first for two freshly cut filets and a medley of vegetables for the side dish.

Once she finally arrived at home, Brandt had less than an hour before Summer's arrival. She changed from her business suit to a casual pair of khaki shorts and a polo shirt. Then, she quickly prepped the steaks and veggies with seasoning and opened a new bottle of wine to let it breathe. Her phone rang at the last minute and she shook her head, seeing Bean's face on the caller ID. She was glad she'd chosen to let the call go to her voicemail since the doorbell rang a few seconds later.

Brandt pulled the front door open and waved for Summer to come in. "Welcome," she said, noticing Summer was in jeans and a halter style top that tied behind her neck. Her shirt dipped into a deep V between her breasts and her upper back was bare under the wavy strands of chestnut colored hair.

"Wow," she murmured, flabbergasted as she walked inside and took a quick look around. "I thought you had a boring job at some low-budget production company."

Brandt led her out to the pool deck, where she poured them both a glass of wine. "Well, I may have understated a little."

"A little?" Summer squeaked, looking out at the breathtaking view of the valley and mountains as she walked around the pool to the rail. "What exactly do you do?"

"B2 is a low-budget production company that makes LGBT movies, or mostly lesbian, to be honest. Our films have won awards at Sundance, Cannes, and other film festivals, as well as numerous LGBT awards."

Summer nodded. "What exactly do you do there?"

Brandt sipped her wine. "I'm a screenwriter and producer," she said, avoiding telling her that she actually owned half of the company she'd founded with her best friend.

Summer hid her surprise between the wine glass, taking several sips.

"It's nothing like working for the big Hollywood studios," Brandt added, stepping up next to her by the rail. "But, I love what I do and live comfortably."

"You're obviously very successful. I'd say this is a little more than comfortable," she murmured, looking back at the pool and the large, modern-style house behind it.

"I worked extremely hard, saving every penny I earned and bought this house with cash money. After that, I was a poor woman living in a million-dollar home. Thankfully, it was in foreclosure when I bought it, so I got a good deal and was able to make all of the upgrades that I wanted, but it took me a few years to get ahead again. I'm not rich by any means, especially compared to my neighbors, but like I said, I live comfortably. I work hard and my films are getting bigger and bigger every year."

"Wow. I had no idea," Summer said, amazed at what she was hearing. She was surprised she hadn't learned all of this on the cruise during the time they spent together, but after everything Brandt had gone through, she didn't blame her for downplaying her career.

Summer sipped the last of her wine as thoughts raced through her mind. She wasn't sure if she could be involved with someone so intertwined with the LGBT community when she was hiding from the world in a straight sheep's clothing to protect her own career.

Brandt watched the emotions play across Summer's face. She'd wanted to tell her more about her life, but their time together had been so short and she wasn't sure she could ever trust anyone again after Jenna's deceitfulness.

"Would you like a refill?" Brandt asked, holding up the wine bottle. "I'm going to go ahead and get dinner going."

Summer took the bottle and added a little more to her glass while Brandt lit the large propane grill. She couldn't deny the attraction between them anymore than she could refute it on the cruise and that scared her. She'd thrown caution to the wind on the ship because she knew she'd probably never see any of those people again. She had been able to finally be herself for once in her life and it had felt wonderful. Spending time with Brandt, snorkeling and exploring a new place had been a lot of fun, and making love with her was seemingly indescribable, but her life in L.A. was completely different from her life on the ship. She had an image to uphold and she wasn't sure where, or even if, Brandt fit in.

Brandt walked into the house and came back out with the marinating steaks in one hand and foil boat full of seasoned veggies in the other. Summer rushed over and closed the door behind her.

"Those look good," she said, peering down at the steaks as Brandt laid them on the hot grating.

Brandt smiled, placing the foil boat on the opposite side. "Would you like to eat out here or inside?"

Summer noticed the sun inching lower towards the mountains and the dark clouds gathering behind it. "Outside so we can watch the sunset—if those clouds don't get here first."

"Sounds good."

Brandt went inside again and returned with two table settings, placing them diagonal from each other on the patio dining set, which sat on the opposite end of the pool deck from the grill. She walked back over, flipping the steaks and stirring the vegetable medley.

"Are you an only child?" Summer asked.

Brandt turned her head, looking at Summer with a grin on her face. "Why do you ask?"

Summer shrugged. "You're very independent. That's a trait most single children pick up."

Brandt nodded. "Yes, I am. You?"

"No. Autumn, my sister, is two years older than me."

"Autumn and Summer." Brandt looked at her quizzically. "Are your parents fans of the seasons?"

Summer laughed, "No, they're hippies."

"What?"

"I'm serious. Vegan-eating, hemp-wearing hippies."

"Wow. That's different," Brandt said, pulling the steaks from the grill.

"No kidding. They aren't potheads anymore, but they were before we were born. When they had Autumn, they made a lot of lifestyle changes and actually bought a house. When I was five, Autumn and I loved dancing and a friend of mine in school was in ballroom dancing. Her mother mentioned it to my parents, who took us to check it out. Autumn and I were hooked and quickly joined. Within a year, we were on the youth ballroom circuit, going to competitions every weekend. My parents sold their house in Oregon and moved us to Berkeley, California, so we could train with the best coaches and, well, still be hippies." She smiled.

Brandt pulled the veggie boat from the grill and took everything over to the table. "That's crazy."

"Yeah, they gave up a lot for us, but they're happy and still try to incorporate the hippie style into the life they have now." Summer placed one of the steaks and some of the veggies onto her plate. "This looks good and smells delicious."

"Here's to living life," Brandt toasted, holding her glass up.

"I'll drink to that." Summer touched their glasses together and took a sip before cutting into her juicy, perfectly cooked steak.

"Is Autumn a pro dancer like you?"

"No, not anymore. She got pregnant not long after joining the pro tour as an adult and married her son's father. They live in San Jose, so they're not too far from my parents. Autumn owns a dance studio where she teaches ballroom dancing to people of all ages. She's happy and she loves what she does. My nephew, Wade, is a dancer too, but he's also into playing rugby like his dad."

Summer lit up when she talked about her family and Brandt couldn't help noticing the difference in her demeanor. She was so natural and pure, completely opposite of the company Brandt usually kept.

"This is wonderful by the way," Summer murmured between bites. "So, what about your family?"

"What about them?" Brandt asked.

"Where do they live?"

"My parents are in New Haven, Connecticut. They're Irish-born science nerds and tenured professors at Yale."

"Wow."

Brandt smiled. "They're quite the opposite of me."

"How did you wind up working with movies?"

"That's a long, boring story."

Summer smiled.

Brandt laughed and continued."They wanted me to follow in their footsteps when I finished high school, but a tenured spot at Yale wasn't my dream. I'd come out to them earlier that year, which threw them for a loop, but they wanted me to be who I was meant to be. So, I decided to go live with my grandmother in Queens and try to find myself. That's where she and my grandfather wound up when their parents migrated in the early 1900s. Both of my parents were from immigrant Irish families and that's how they met. Anyway, I wound up going to college in New York and wasn't sure what I wanted to do, but I loved writing, so I settled on English as my major."

The sun began to set behind the mountain, casting a bright orange glow over the valley.

"This view is breathtaking," Summer murmured.

"Yes. It's what sold me on the house. I knew as soon as I saw it that this was where I wanted to live my life."

Summer locked eyes with her and smiled. "So, how did you become a screenwriter and producer?"

"I'd written a few short stories by my sophomore year, one of which was published. By the end of my senior year, I met this eccentric, nerdy woman named Bean Pratt. She was a film director and she and I made my published story into a short film. It won a couple of awards, one of which came with a screenwriting grant to a prestigious film school. I spent the next two years learning all about screenwriting, then I went to work for a small production company as a screenwriter after that."

"Brandt, your story is incredible." Summer reached across the table, running her hand over the top of Brandt's. "What brought you to Cali?" she asked, pulling her hand away.

"Bean and I became best friends and we moved out here together to follow our dream of making movies for people like us. So, we took mediocre jobs at film studios, me as an assistant screenwriter and her as an assistant director. Bean's ten years older than me, so she already had a lot of experience with films. Seven years ago, I wrote a screenplay that she directed. We produced it ourselves and it was an instant hit. We used the money to fund B2 pictures, and well, here I am, six years later."

Summer sat back, completely enthralled as she pushed her empty plate aside. "I had no idea you were so…I don't know, talented, intriguing, smart." She shook her head.

"Thank you, but the story sounds a lot more glamorous than it is. We bust our asses working a lot of hours and travel more days than we're home sometimes, but the pay-off in the end is doing what we love. It's definitely cost us things along the way, that's for sure— the latest being my non-existent marriage."

"If your ex didn't see you for who you are, then she's stupid and you're better off without someone like that in your life." Summer looked into the Brandt's blue eyes.

Brandt sipped the last of her wine and smiled at the beautiful woman looking back at her. Summer was sexy as hell, there was no denying it, especially when she was dancing, but there was also a vulnerable side to her that drew Brandt in even further.

Brandt broke the intense stare and carried some of the dishes into the house. Summer followed, carrying the rest of them. No words were spoken as Brandt stepped back outside, making sure the grill was off. She moved to pick up the nearly empty wine bottle, but Summer came up beside her, reaching at the same time. Their hands met in the semi-darkness and Brandt pulled her close, kissing Summer with everything she had built up inside of her.

Summer returned the passionate kiss at first, but then pulled away, putting some distance between them. "I'm sorry," she murmured, turning away. "I can't do this."

Brandt watched her walk into the house and heard the car drive away a minute later. She shook her head and sat on the chaise lounge, chugging the last of the wine.

Chapter 19

Brandt sat outside, staring up at the stars until the dark clouds finally rolled in nearly an hour after Summer had abruptly left. She felt the first heavy drops of rain on her skin and scurried inside. By the time she closed the door, thunder and lightning had begun to rattle the windows as heavy sheets of rain poured down. She went into the kitchen and washed the dishes, then headed up to take a hot shower.

Two hours later, Brandt was lounging on her couch in a t-shirt and running shorts, skimming through the channels on the TV, when the doorbell rang. She sat up, wondering who would be at her door this late at night since it was close to eleven and still storming like crazy. One thing was for certain, whoever it was had the code to the gate.

Brandt walked into the kitchen and checked the loaded gun she kept in the side drawer under the appliance manuals. Satisfied that it was ready if she needed it, she walked over and flipped the outside light on as she looked through the peephole. Summer was on the other side of the door, shielding her eyes. She was soaked to the bone and looked like a waterlogged, drowned rat. Brandt yanked the door open and pulled her inside quickly.

"Hold on," Brandt said, running across the dark wood floors to the get a towel from the bathroom. She returned seconds later with freshly laundered, fluffy towel, which she wrapped around her. Summer's cheeks and eyes were red, obviously from crying. "Are you okay?" she asked.

"I'm sorry I ran away and that I keep running." Summer shook her head and turned her eyes up to Brandt. "I'm falling in love with you and I don't know what to do."

Brandt stepped closer, cupping Summer's cool cheeks with her hands and kissing her softly. Then, she pulled away slightly, looking into Summer's pale green eyes.

"I'm not going to chase you," she murmured.

"I'm done running," Summer whispered.

"I don't have the strength to get my heart broken…especially not by you," Brandt sighed, knowing the feelings she had for Summer were nothing like the love she thought she'd felt for Jenna. It was so much stronger, nearly burning her to the core.

"I won't break your heart," Summer said softly, leaning in and pressing her lips to Brandt's.

Brandt returned the slow, lingering kiss as she moved her hands down Summer's body, grasping the hands at her waist. She ended the kiss and tugged the smaller woman along as she headed up the stairs. Summer had never seen the rest of the house, but she wasn't about to stop now to check it out as she followed Brandt into her bedroom. The vertical blinds over the French doors to the small balcony were turned, allowing the flashes of lightening to bounce around the room.

Lightening cracked loud in the distance with every burst of light.

Brandt pulled Summer's wet clothes from her skin, tossing them to the floor behind her as she ran her lips and tongue over the cool, wet skin in front of her. Summer gasped and bit her lower lip as Brandt licked and sucked her breasts, moving lower until Summer was naked and Brandt's mouth was between her legs.

Summer put her hands on the back of Brandt's head in her hair, grinding against her face as her body lost control way too quickly. Brandt smiled and held onto Summer's shaky body as she kissed her way back up to Summer's lips, trading a few passionate kisses before Brandt grabbed Summer's hand and moved towards the bed. They lay down together on their sides, kissing and touching each other with languid strokes.

Brandt sat up in the middle of the bed. "Come here," she said, urging Summer to her knees to straddle her lap.

When Summer moved over her, Brandt put one hand between them, sliding two fingers deep inside of her with her other arm around Summer's waist. Summer moaned and bit her lower lip as she slid herself up and down slowly on Brandt's fingers. She tangled one hand in Brandt's short hair and wrapped the other around her shoulders as their lips met passionately once again.

Summer rode back and forth, faster and harder, pushing Brandt's fingers deeper inside of her until she slipped over the edge into ecstasy. Brandt held her with one arm while she felt the wet muscles constrict her fingers over and over until Summer's orgasm had passed.

Summer stayed in Brandt's lap until her body had relaxed, then she pushed Brandt to her back and quickly slid down, running her tongue in long, hard strokes over Brandt's clit. She pushed her wavy curls over her shoulder, but they fell over Brandt's waist and thigh, enticing her even more. Brandt didn't think there was anything sexier than another woman's long hair fanning over her body as they made love.

Brandt gasped and clutched at the sheets as her body betrayed her, giving Summer the quick release she wanted. Then, Summer wasted no time, sliding her fingers deep inside of Brandt before she'd even recovered, nearly bringing her to a second orgasm. Brandt lifted her hips, urging Summer deeper as her body began to tighten once more. After a few deep strokes, Brandt's body released the tension it had built as she let out a guttural moan. Summer smiled and pulled her fingers free before kissing Brandt one last time and curling up against her.

~

The next morning, Brandt woke up to the smell of coffee. She was alone in the bed and the space next to her was cold. She got out of the bed, pulling on a t-shirt and pair of shorts, before heading down the stairs.

Summer was sitting at the island in the middle of the kitchen wearing one of Brandt's t-shirts and an old pair of shorts with her hair up haphazardly in a makeshift bun that had loose strands falling down. She was drinking coffee while scrolling social media on her phone. Brandt leaned against the entranceway, watching her. She wasn't sure what the future held for them, and truth be told, she wasn't sure if she wanted to go all-in on another relationship, especially when the last one had just ended less than a month ago, but Brandt had a strong feeling she was already too far gone to turn back now. The sight of the beautiful woman sitting in her kitchen, wearing her clothes with nothing under them, made her weak in the knees all over again. She turned to go take a shower instead of devouring the sexy body a few feet away.

"Good morning, sleepyhead." Summer grinned. "I made coffee a few minutes ago, so it's probably still hot."

"Oh, it's definitely hot," Brandt whispered, stepping into the kitchen. She walked over, kissing Summer softly before going to the coffeemaker.

"I hope you don't mind, I borrowed some clothes."

"No, not at all." Brandt eyed the clothes that were about two sizes too big. She found the tousled look sexy on her.

Summer watched Brandt pour herself a cup of coffee, wincing at the amount of cream and sugar she added to it. "Why not just drink a glass of sugar milk?" Summer teased.

"Easy," Brandt warned with a smile.

Summer laughed as Brandt joined her at the island. "I was going to make breakfast, but there wasn't much to choose from," she said.

"Yeah, I usually grab coffee and a muffin or a bagel in the morning on my way to the office. On the weekends, I eat cereal and sometimes I'll make a smoothie with frozen fruit, but I didn't go to the grocery store this week."

"I can tell. Your refrigerator's pretty bare."

"I'm leaving tomorrow for Vancouver and I'll be gone about three weeks, so that's why I haven't shopped."

"What are you doing up there?" Summer asked, sipping her coffee.

"Shooting a new movie."

"Wow. That's exciting," Summer exclaimed.

"What about you? When does the show start?"

"A week and a half. We meet our partners on Monday."

"That should be fun."

Summer forced a smile.

"What's wrong?" Brandt asked. She knew they needed to talk and had a feeling that's what was coming. She grabbed Summer's hand and walked to the couch in the living room where they sat down together.

"Only a small percentage of dancers are able to make a career out of doing what they love and I've worked so hard to be successful." Summer bit her lower lip and curled her legs under her. "I've sacrificed so much, pushing everything aside," she sighed.

"I know the entertainment industry is difficult. You don't have to tell me that." Brandt brushed aside a loose piece of hair from Summer's face.

"I hide in the closet and date men to keep up appearances. I've gone as far as pushing myself to be straight. I recently broke up with the guy I was in a relationship with for two years."

"Summer, that's crazy. You should be who you are," Brandt said, shaking her head.

"It's not that easy. Especially not now that I'm going into the spotlight on this popular TV show," Summer sighed. "It's different for you—you work in the

LGBT industry. Dancing has a totally different following."

"Where does this leave us?" Brandt asked.

"I'm telling you all of this so you know what my life is like. I want to be with you, Brandt, but I need you to understand how different things are for me. I have to stay deeply hidden in the closet to protect my career."

Brandt wrapped her arms around Summer, pulling her close. "I'm not going to tell you that I like any of this. I'd be lying." Brandt kissed her forehead and sighed. "I'll do whatever you want me to do," she said, seemingly agreeing to keep Summer's secret and pretend they were only friends. She'd just taken a giant step back from all of the progress she'd made as a successful, out and proud lesbian woman.

Summer wrapped her arms around Brandt's waist and melded into the warm body against her. She wiped a stray tear from her cheek, knowing this was a huge sacrifice for Brandt.

"Thank you," Summer whispered.

Brandt held her tight and slightly prayed she wasn't making the biggest mistake of her life.

Chapter 20

Over the next two weeks, Brandt ran around the B&B like a headless chicken as they began filming the first set of scenes for the movie. Bean sometimes hated when they were filming one of Brandt's movies because, as the screenwriter, the story was like her baby and she was unwilling to let go. As the director, it was Bean's job to manage the entire set on top of making sure every scene was perfect. Brandt needed to give up her role as the screenwriter and put on her producer hat in order to get the movie filmed with the best quality shots and on schedule.

"What's gotten into you?" Bean asked as they wrapped the first week. "You're jumpier than usual."

"I don't know. The budget for this picture is one of the highest and I guess I want to make sure it's perfect and preferably under budget," Brandt lied. She hated not telling her best friend that she was secretly dating the most amazing person she'd ever met. It had only been a week, but the secret was eating away at her.

"It'll be fine. This week went great and we're shooting all weekend, so we'll be back ahead of schedule at this rate."

Brandt smiled. "I know. This is where you tell me to trust you."

"Exactly." Bean grinned as she adjusted her glasses. "Do you want to go grab a drink?"

"Nah, I need to make some calls. I'll catch up with you later," Brandt replied, stepping away.

She walked out of the B&B and headed down the gravel drive as she pulled her phone from her pocket, scrolling through the contacts. The sun was just starting to set and she watched it drop over the horizon as she continued down the path.

"Hey," Summer answered. "I was just thinking about you."

"I hope they were good thoughts. How was your first week of the show?"

"It was crazy, that's for sure. Did you watch it?"

"No, it wasn't on here. The place we're staying only has a couple of network channels—the rest are cable channels. I watched bits and pieces of it on YouTube. You looked beautiful and the dancing was incredible, at least what I was able to see."

"I'm partnered with a guy named Jorge. He's a deli owner from New York City. He's nice and seems to be getting the steps down. We'll see how it goes. Jive definitely wasn't his strong suit. Our dance next week is the foxtrot."

"Is that fast or slow?" Brandt asked.

"It's a traditional ballroom dance with long, fluid motions—kind of like the waltz."

"Sounds interesting."

"It's odd being in two different countries at the moment," Summer laughed. "I wish I could see you, but even if you were here, I probably couldn't see you. I've been so busy, I don't know whether I'm coming or going some days. Jorge and I have been in the studio for six

145

hours a day, then I'm rehearsing with the troupe for three to four hours a day. Throw in wardrobe fittings, camera blocking, and commercial shoots for the show and I've barely had any time to sleep."

"Wow, and I thought I had a long week! Is it going to be like this for the entire ten weeks?"

"It's more like 18 weeks of chaos when you count the before and after weeks," Summer sighed. "I miss you. It was so quiet and peaceful at your house before all of this started."

"It sounds like you miss my house," Brandt teased.

"Well, that too," Summer laughed. "Are you going to be at the show next week?"

"No, I have too much going on here, but I plan to fly down for the one after that."

"Great. I'll make sure to leave your tickets at the door, and when it's over, I'll give you a backstage tour."

"Sounds like a plan."

"I need to get going. I have a meeting to get to."

"It's Friday night," Brandt said.

"The producers of the show don't care," Summer laughed. "I'll talk to you soon."

Brandt hung up her phone and walked back up the gravel path that was mostly lit by the moonlight, with a little bit of illumination coming from the driveway markers. She heard a few giggles nearby and cut across the grass to see what was going on.

"Everyone's going to know what we're up to," Bean giggled.

"So? They're all adults—they'll understand," Misty whispered, kissing her.

Brandt stood a few feet away with her arms crossed over her chest, shaking her head at the two women making out against the side of the building like teenagers. They both spun around with their eyes wide when she cleared her throat loudly.

"We…uh…" Bean stammered.

"Got caught," Brandt laughed, finishing her sentence.

Bean pushed her glasses up and crossed her arms like a defiant kid who just got scolded.

"I'll leave you kids alone." Brandt smiled, seeing the embarrassment on her best friends face. Brandt loved Bean to death and knew she was as sexually active as most people her age and had no problem talking about sex or shooting sex scenes for a movie, but she was so shy when it came to her own life that it made her act like the forty-year-old virgin sometimes. "So, you know there are actual bedrooms inside if that wall gets too uncomfortable," Brandt teased as she walked away.

She headed down to the bench near the shore and sat down, tossing pebbles into the water. The ache she felt deep down was something she never experienced when she and Jenna were together, yet they loved each other and were happy—or at least, that's what she thought. The feelings she had for Summer were obviously on a completely different wavelength. She wondered if part of it was because she couldn't share her happiness with anyone else.

~

A week and a half later, Brandt rushed from the set after their afternoon shoot and hopped a plane for the three-hour flight back to L.A. As soon as she arrived, she grabbed a taxi and headed to the studio lot where the show was filmed. A large line of people were wrapped around the building and slowly being let in through the double doors. Brandt paid the driver for her fare and walked up to the security men standing at the door.

"I'm supposed to have a ticket waiting for me that one of the pro dancers left," she said.

"The private celebrity entrance is around the corner," one of the men directed her.

"Oh, okay. Thanks." She didn't feel like a celebrity, but apparently that's where she was sitting, so she added a little pep in her step as she walked around to the private entrance.

Three of Hollywood's biggest celebrities were walking in when she spotted the door. Brandt walked up behind them and showed her ID to the security guard at the door. He pointed the direction for her to go to get her ticket, which she quickly did, and then she headed to her seat on the side of the stage in the second row. She was surprised to see all of the famous people sitting around her.

After half an hour, the house lights went down and the host of the show took center stage. Brandt watched as each of the couples were introduced and walked out onto the stage together. She smiled when she saw Summer dressed in a red corset with black mesh over it, forming a blouse, and a black, mesh-covered chiffon skirt that had a slit all the way up to her hip on one side. Her partner, Jorge, was dressed like a matador, also in red and black. The other couples were similarly dressed for the Paso Doble dance of the night. As soon as the couples disappeared, the show went to a commercial and came back on with the troupe of pro dancers pairing up for an elegant waltz. Brandt was surprised at how quickly they'd changed clothes during the quick break.

Summer looked more beautiful than ever in the long silver beaded chiffon dress with her hair flowing in spiral waves down her back and swaying behind her. The pairs circled the floor as the song played, and then they rushed off the stage as the host announced the first couple. The male pro only had to change his jacket before coming back out onto the floor with his average partner.

Brandt watched closely as they danced the fast and slow, pristine movements of the Latin dance. She wasn't a trained eye when it came to the dance, but she was sure she noticed a few missteps. Two more couples came out, doing their versions of the same dance, before Summer and Jorge took the stage.

Annie Lennox's version of "I Put A Spell On You" played as they danced the intricate dance. Summer looked sexy as hell in the role of the seductress, taking control as the matador and making her male partner follow her. Their dance was very non-traditional and exciting, drawing huge cheers from the crowd. Brandt smiled and clapped. Summer was truly incredible when it came to dancing and her choreography was simply genius. When the song ended, the crowd rose to their feet, clapping loudly and whistling.

The rest of the hour-long show finished with more troupe dances and three more pairs. Once it was over, the people around her began leaving and Brandt waited behind for Summer to come out.

"Excuse me, are you with Summer Durham?" a man with a clipboard asked.

"What?" Brandt said, raising an eyebrow.

"Are you a guest of one of the pro dancers?" he asked again.

"Oh, yeah. Sorry. I misheard you." Brandt said, following him to the area backstage where all of the dancers were peeling out of their costumes in the dressing rooms.

"Ms. Durham will be out in a moment," the man said before walking away.

The door opened a minute later and Summer was standing there in baggy warm up pants and a tank top over a sports bra. She resembled the woman Brandt had first met at the coffee shop and then at the scene of their accident.

"Hey!" Summer exclaimed. "What did you think?"

"It's was great!" Brandt smiled. She wanted nothing more than to pull the smaller woman into her arms and kiss her passionately, but bit her lip nearly to the point of making it bleed as she reverted to the role of simply a friend. "I really liked it," she said.

Summer smiled brightly. "Come on, I'll show you around."

Brandt walked around with her as Summer introduced her as a friend to Jorge and the other pro dancers and showed what went on behind the scenes. Brandt was familiar with camera equipment, but it was neat to see how a live show was filmed. She was used to filming the scene a few times over and then watching the playback to see which take was the best. So, she'd spent a portion of the show watching the camera angles.

When they were finished with the tour, Summer grabbed her gym bag and lead Brandt to the parking area in the back lot where her car was located. "Did you drive here?" she asked.

"No. I came straight from the airport, so I took a cab."

"When do you have to go back?" Summer asked, hitting the keyless entry on her SUV.

Brandt slid into the passenger seat. "My return flight is at eleven."

"In the morning?" Summer started the vehicle and pulled out of the parking lot.

"Tonight," Brandt corrected.

"What? Brandt, that's in less than an hour," Summer huffed.

"I know. It's a three-hour flight and the first flight out tomorrow isn't until ten in the morning. I wouldn't get there until the afternoon. I plan to stay overnight next time. I didn't realize I'd be cutting it so close."

"Well, if I'd known you were flying right back, I wouldn't have wasted time showing you around."

"Can you pull over?" Brandt questioned.

Summer turned into a parking lot and turned the car off. "What's wrong?"

Brandt unbuckled her seatbelt and leaned over the console, kissing Summer hard. Summer pulled her own seatbelt away and wrapped her arms around Brandt, pulling her closer.

"God, I've missed you," Summer panted. "Damn you for leaving so soon."

"I hate it too. But Summer, this is our life. We both have demanding careers that allow for stolen moments and occasional weekends. If this isn't going to work for you, then you need to tell me now while this is still new."

"No. I know it sucks, but I understand," Summer said, kissing her again. "I know it won't always be like this."

"How about instead of coming to the next show, I come home for the weekend?"

Summer grinned. "Yes. I'd rather have you all night than know you're sitting in the audience where I can't touch you."

"Alright, it's a plan. Now, get me to the airport before I miss my flight."

Summer laughed and resituated herself in the driver's seat.

Chapter 21

Over the next three weeks, Brandt and Bean worked diligently filming their movie. Bean and Misty continued to sneak around for no apparent reason. Everyone on the set knew they were filming a lesbian movie and everyone knew Bean was a lesbian. Brandt thought her best friend's shyness was cute, but it only made her more agitated about having to hide her own relationship. Thankfully, they only had two more weeks of filming; then, Brandt and Bean would be back in the office working with Viv to edit all of the shots and paste them together to make a movie.

Summer and her dance partner, Jorge, went through a bad week on the show with the cha-cha. She simply couldn't get his hips to move, but they redeemed themselves the following week with a nearly perfect Viennese waltz and then a good Tango the week after that. They were halfway through the ten-week season and the pair was steadily in the middle, floating between number three and four with the voting each week. They needed to be in the top three in week nine in order to dance in the final week for a chance to win the show. Summer was under a lot of pressure to perform well and have a strong finish to the season since she was the newest pro dancer. She'd also started building a huge fan base. People were starting to stop her at the store and in the coffee shop to take pictures with her and have her sign autographs. She was surprised and had never anticipated that kind of personal following. She knew people watched and followed the show, of course, but her social media pages had picked up a few thousand likes and follows in five weeks' time.

It didn't help matters that Lewis, Summer's ex-boyfriend, had gotten back in touch with her and had been to a couple of the shows. At first, he'd told her how much he still cared for her, but after Summer told him they'd never be anything more than friends, he seemed to accept that.

~

The movie wrapped nearly a week early and Brandt flew back to L.A. on the next flight out. She got her car from the airport valet and headed to the dance studio to surprise Summer since she was home a week early. Summer and Jorge had just wrapped up and she was in the studio alone, working on the next bit of their choreography, when Brandt walked in. Summer didn't hear her over the music, so Brandt leaned against the wall, watching her move gracefully around the floor. Summer was wearing a sports bra with a sleeveless t-shirt over that had long slits cut in the sides, and black legging-style dance pants with sneakers. Her wavy hair was up in a messy ponytail with a few loose strands dangling down next to her face. When she stopped to redo the same steps she'd just laid out, Summer saw Brandt's reflection in the mirror and her face lit up like a kid at Christmas. She spun around, ran across the room, and jumped into Brandt's arms.

"Oh, my God," Summer squealed. "How long are you here?" she asked between kisses.

Brandt set Summer back on her feet and kept her arms loosely around her waist. "Until we film the next movie or I go to a screening or something." She smiled.

"Are you serious? I thought production didn't wrap until next week."

"We finished early and I wanted to see you." Brandt grinned.

Summer wrapped her arms around Brandt's neck and pulled her down for a searing kiss. Brandt ran her hands under Summer's shirt to the sweat-soaked skin of her back.

"Oh, yuck!" Brandt grimaced.

Summer laughed. "I literally just finished a six-hour rehearsal. I need a shower."

"Oh, that could be fun," Brandt teased.

"I'm also starving. I feel like I haven't eaten since yesterday."

"Again...fun." Brandt smiled.

Summer laughed. "Come on, I'll go to my place so I can shower and then you can pick me up so we can go to dinner somewhere."

Brandt nodded and walked out with her.

~

During their dinner, Summer was asked to take pictures with two different people. She kindly obliged before sitting back down to finish her meal. Brandt knew she'd picked up more of a celebrity status from being on the show, but she hadn't seen it with her own eyes because she'd been away so much.

"Do you want to order dessert?" Summer asked.

"Are you on the menu?" Brandt teased.

Summer shook her head and laughed.

They walked out of the upscale, West Hollywood restaurant a few minutes later and a paparazzo walked up. "Ms. Durham, how long have you known Brandt Coghlan? You are Brandt Coghlan, the award winning lesbian film writer and producer, yes?" he asked.

"What?" Brandt said, walking around him to get into her car.

"Are you two just friends or is there more to you hanging out together?" he asked Summer. "Brandt's been seen in the audience at *Anyone Can Dance* and you've been photographed together on more than one outing."

"We're just friends," Summer replied. "Can't people simply have friends anymore?" she growled as she got into the passenger seat of Brandt's car. "Can you believe that guy?" she sneered as Brandt drove away.

"It was bound to happen. You're getting more and more known with that show. People are going to start recognizing you everywhere you go. Now, me—no one knows who I am in this city unless they look up my name or one of my movies."

"Why can't they just accept that we're friends?"

"Because we're not," Brandt answered.

Summer shook her head. They'd been having a great time a dinner and she was so happy to have Brandt back in town, but the asshole paparazzi guy had completely ruined her evening.

Brandt pulled up outside of Summer's apartment building and checked the mirror to see if they'd been followed.

"Stay the night with me," Summer whispered, running her fingers over Brandt's hand.

"There's nothing I'd rather do," Brandt replied softly.

~

Summer's one-bedroom apartment was on the third floor of a small apartment building. When they walked in, Brandt immediately noticed how small and tidy the space was. The open kitchen was to the left with a petite dining table on the right. Further back from there was the living area with a couch, coffee table and TV stand. The bedroom and bathroom were to the left and off the kitchen. Her office upstairs in her house was bigger than the entire apartment.

"It's not much, but rent out here is ridiculous. I can afford something bigger, especially now that I'm on the show, but I'm not here much anyway and it's easy to keep clean." Summer kicked off her heels and unzipped the back of the short black dress she'd been wearing. "How do you keep your place so clean?" she asked, stepping into the bedroom to change clothes.

Brandt removed her suit jacket and rolled her cuffs back as she followed her. "I get serviced once a week," Brandt replied in a sultry voice as she walked up behind her, pushing the straps from her shoulders.

Summer grinned as she shimmied out of the dress and turned to face her wearing only a black satin bra and matching thong panties. "I guess we're going to sleep now, since you've already been serviced this week," she teased as she slid her hand over Brandt's breast and up her chest to the back of her neck.

Brandt said nothing as she grabbed Summer's hands, pulling her arms from around her neck and turning Summer around before pulling the smaller woman back against her. She wrapped one arm around her upper chest, slipping it inside the cup of her bra to squeeze and massage her breast. Then, she rubbed her crotch against Summer's ass, kissing her neck next to her ear as she moved her other hand over Summer's hip to her tight stomach and under the front of her thong, dipping into the wetness between her legs.

Summer gasped softly as Brandt's fingers worked back and forth slowly over her hard clit. Brandt held Summer tightly against her body, rocking with her as she hissed and panted. Summer ran her hand back over Brandt's neck and into her hair, tugging the short tendrils, and she rubbed her ass harder into her crotch. Brandt kept her movements slow and deliberate, backing off each time she felt Summer get close to her release.

"Please," Summer begged.

"Please what?" Brandt whispered in her ear as she ran her tongue around the outside of it.

Summer swallowed the lump in her throat. "Let me cum," she panted.

"Is that what you want?" Brandt murmured, biting the lobe of her ear.

"Yes," Summer pleaded breathlessly.

Brandt rubbed her clit harder and Summer moaned loudly as Brandt slipped her fingers inside of her, before pulling them back out to circled her clit with perfectly timed strokes.

158

Summer lost control, crying out and shuddering in Brandt's arms as the waves of orgasm tore through her body. Brandt moved her hand to Summer's stomach, holding her close as her body went slightly limp. Summer turned in her arms, kissing Brandt like a long-lost lover, before moving to her knees, dragging her hands down Brandt's body along the way. She stopped at her crotch, opening the button and zipper and grabbing her panties to push everything down—enough for her to get her mouth on Brandt's swollen clit.

Brandt held her breath as she held Summer's hair with one hand and pushed her face into her crotch with the other, moving her hips to guide her as Summer licked her with long, wide strokes.

"Yeah, baby," Brandt panted as her body began to tighten.

Summer grinned as she slowed teasing her with a circular path to slow down the impending release. Two could definitely play this seductive game of who was going to give in first. Brandt tried to move her hips where she wanted Summer's mouth, but Summer changed directions. Brandt grunted as Summer bit her softly, then moved her tongue right where Brandt needed it, bringing her over the edge with a few hard licks.

Brandt nearly lost her footing as she tried to hold on long enough for Summer to finish her off. When Summer's mouth finally stilled, Brandt pulled her to her feet in one swift motion, wrapping her arms around her and meeting her lips in a deeply passionate kiss, reveling in the taste of herself on Summer's tongue.

Summer pulled away, looking into her eyes as she ran her hand over Brandt's cheek. "I love you," she said softly. It was the first time she'd said those three words first to someone and the only time she'd ever whole-heartedly meant it.

Brandt closed her eyes, feeling the warm hand on her face. "I love you too," she murmured, opening her eyes to see Summer staring back at her. She'd never felt anything as powerful as that single moment.

They slowly made their way over to the bed, shedding clothes and trading kisses before falling on top of the comforter in a heap of arms and legs.

Chapter 22

At the end of the week before the show finale, Brandt was sitting in the editing room with Viv, going through slides of the movie they were working on, when her cell phone rang. Seeing that it was Summer, she excused herself from the room and walked down the hall to her office.

"Hey," she answered.

"Brandt, I don't know what to do," Summer said frantically.

"What? Calm down. What's going on?"

"There are pictures of us together floating around the internet and TMZ did some fucking story this morning on us. I don't know what to do. People are asking questions."

"I'm sorry, babe. I had a feeling this would happen. You have a big following from the show because you're an incredible dancer and everyone adores you." Brandt looked up at the movie posters on her wall and sighed. "Just stick to your story and tell them we're friends."

"I don't think that's good enough. Maybe I should be seen out with a guy—they'll think we're dating."

"Summer, that's not the best idea."

"Well, I don't know what else to do. This is my career we're talking about. The whole world already knows you're gay, so it's no big deal to you," she snapped.

Brandt rubbed her temple, trying to delay the headache she knew was coming. "Why don't you take a step back, go home and take a hot bath to relax, and you and I will talk about all of this tonight."

"I'm in the middle of rehearsal. Jorge went to go grab some lunch and I stayed in the studio to work on some of my troupe choreography," Summer paused, wiping a tear from her cheek. "I don't know how to deal with this. I'm not ready, I'm sorry."

Brandt heard the sadness in her voice and it made her angry that she couldn't make this mess go away for Summer. "I'll stand behind whatever you decide to do," she said, knowing she wasn't going to like the outcome.

"Brandt, you don't know how much that means to me. I love you."

"I love you too," Brandt said. She leaned back in her chair as the call ended, staring around the room at all of her accomplishments, from the movies she'd written and produced, to the awards she'd won for them.

~

"Trouble in paradise?" Viv asked when Brandt joined her once again.

"Huh?" Brandt raised an eyebrow.

"I'm up to date with all of the latest Hollywood gossip. How long have you and Summer Durham been checking each other's oil? She's hot by the way. I'm a huge fan of the show."

Brandt shook her head. "We're just friends. Those idiots saw us having lunch and dinner together a couple of times and now they think we're screwing. I'm so sick of Hollywood and all of the bullshit that goes with it," she growled.

"I'm sorry," Viv replied, going back to the matter at hand. "I think we should pause on this scene here. It builds on the main character plotting her next step."

"Run it both ways and let me see it," Brandt said.

They spent the next three hours going over the movie section by section. When Brandt felt like her eyes were going to pop out, she called it a day and headed out.

"Hey!" Bean called after her as soon as she'd left the building.

"I thought you weren't coming back after your dental appointment?" Brandt said, turning around.

"I got here about a half hour ago. My mouth feels like it's as big as a baseball, but I need to get the promo material finished for the new movie. Are you leaving for the day?"

"Yeah."

"What's going on with you and that dancer?"

Brandt hated lying to her best friend. "We're just friends," she sighed.

"Is she the girl from the cruise?"

Brandt nodded.

"Wait...isn't that the same girl who crashed into you and—"

"Yes, and we're just friends. Those assholes made a story out of nothing, which is what they're known best for doing."

"Alright. I'm going to finish this promo and head home. My mouth's starting to hurt."

"Sounds good. We'll go over it in the morning."

~

Brandt had taken a dip in her pool, then a long soak in the hot tub, before going inside to work on her newest script. She'd already made plot notes on her idea and was in the beginning process of building her characters. She loved this part—creating the people that would eventually come to life on screen.

Brandt was so enthralled in her work that she almost missed the doorbell ringing. She rushed down the stairs. She figured it was Bean coming to find out what was really going on, since she was sure she didn't accept the "friends" story Brandt had given her.

"Hey," she said, surprised as she pulled the door open.

"Were you expecting someone else?" Summer asked.

"No, but I didn't think I'd see you this evening. You sounded pretty busy earlier."

Summer wrapped her arms around Brandt and laid her head on her shoulder.

"I know all of this sucks," Brandt said, holding her tight. "I wish I could make it all go away for you."

"I have a plan," Summer stated, leaning back to look into Brandt's blue eyes.

"Okay."

"I talked to my ex-boyfriend, Lewis, and I explained to him that we'd never be together again, but I need to correct the press, so I asked him to go on a few fake dates with me."

"Summer, this is ridiculous."

"I know you think I should just come out, but I could lose everything. I've been dancing since I was five years old."

"What if you lose nothing?"

"How can you be sure that would happen?"

"I can't."

"Exactly," Summer sighed.

"I'm not thrilled about any of this."

"It won't be long. The finale is in a few days and my name will fade to the back of everyone's minds, hopefully. During the off season, any paparazzi floating around will see Lewis and I together here and there and hopefully move onto someone else."

Brandt sighed in frustration. "I was planning to throw you a wrap party here at the house next Friday night."

"You were?" Summer smiled.

"Yes. This is huge for you and I'm proud of you for making it to the finale. Win or lose, I think it's a cause for celebration."

"That's a great idea. I'll let everyone know."

"Make sure you invite this Lewis guy."

"It's all fake. Trust me, I never wanted to have sex with him when I dated him for real."

"Speaking of sex..." Brandt grinned.

"Aunt Flo arrived today," Summer replied.

"Oh, never mind," Brandt grimaced, causing Summer to laugh. "How about I order delivery and we can curl up on the couch in front of the TV?"

"That sounds like a wonderful idea." Summer smiled.

Chapter 23

The finale of the show had been spectacular. There were multiple troupe dances, most of which Summer and the rest of the pro women were scantily dressed in sexy costumes that revealed way too much skin and the pro men were shirtless. Brandt loved watching Summer perform, but the lack of clothing in front of the entire world made her a little uneasy. The rest of the show had been great, with each of the pairs dancing three different dances—one they chose, one the judges chose, and then a freestyle dance.

Jorge's knee had started to bother him in the previous week, which continued into the finale. It swelled throughout the night, and by the time they set to do their last dance, he could barely bend it. Nevertheless, he pushed through and completed the dance, but the struggle he'd been having with his leg was obvious and they wound up finishing third.

The producers had been extremely happy with Summer's performance throughout the entire season, which made her happy—not to mention, she received a huge bonus for making it to the finale.

~

The following Friday night, Brandt opened her house to nearly thirty guests for the wrap party of the show. She'd invited Bean, along with a few Hollywood producers she knew from working in the industry. Once all of the pro dancers and average partners arrived, the party was in full swing.

"This is quite a turnout," Bean acknowledged, sipping a glass of wine on the pool deck.

"Yeah, I'd expected about twenty people," Brandt replied.

"Hi," one of the male pro dancers said from Brandt's side. She looked at the well-built man with dark hair, slicked back in the ponytail he always wore. He was one of the seasoned veterans on the show and also one of the dancers she'd seen Brandt cutting up with backstage.

She smiled, stepping aside with him by the rail.

"I'm Pierre." He grinned, holding out his hand. "I've seen you backstage a few times with Summer."

"Brandt Coghlan," she added, returning the shake as one of the other female pro dancers walked up.

"This is India," Pierre stated.

Brandt looked at the sultry woman with long, straight black hair, dark eyes, and tanned skin. She looked every bit the seductress she played on the dance floor. She was another one of the dancers Brandt had seen Summer talking with and also the winner of the show.

"It's nice to meet you both," Brandt exclaimed.

"The pleasure is ours." India smiled. "Can I ask how you know Summer?"

"We're good friends," Brandt answered.

India nodded. "Okay." She nodded. "Thank you for throwing this party for all of us."

167

"You're welcome. Congratulations, by the way."

India smiled and winked before she walked away.

Brandt saw Summer come through the French doors wearing a black mini-dress with her hair pushed forward over one shoulder, and holding hands with the guy at her side. He had a small build and was only about an inch or two taller than Brandt, with brown hair and boyish good looks.

"That must be Summer's man. I've seen him backstage a few times too," Pierre said, following her line of sight.

"Pardon me." Brandt nodded, before walking across the pool deck.

"There you are." Summer smiled, stepping closer. "Brandt, this is Lewis Keen."

"It's nice to meet you," he said.

"Likewise." Brandt forced a smile.

"Thank you so much for throwing this party. Everyone's having a great time."

"Yes, I just met India and Pierre. They seem nice."

Summer grinned. "They helped me out a lot. I love them both."

"I want to introduce you to some friends of mine."

"I'll catch up with you in a minute," Summer said to Lewis.

Brandt walked inside where Bean was standing, talking to the two producers she'd invited.

"Summer, this is my best friend and business partner, Bean Pratt, and these guys are Harris Raulerson and Bernie McKindrick."

"It's nice to meet all of you. Ms. Pratt, I've heard a lot about you."

"Likewise." Bean smiled.

Summer turned her eyes to Brandt and she shook her head softly, letting her know their secret was safe.

"Harris and Bernie work for Maxim Pictures and they're fans of the show."

"Oh, wow. That's great."

"I told them you were looking at choreographing for movies down the road and they wanted to meet you."

"It sounds like you have a lot of ambition," Harris said to Summer. "You're an amazing dancer. My wife and I were pulling for you to win the whole thing."

"Aww, thank you." Summer smiled brightly.

"My husband is a huge fan of the show. If I'd known Kelvin Clark was going to be here, I would've brought him."

Kelvin was another one of the male pro dancers and the only other dancer besides India and Pierre that Summer had become friends with. He was very well built with a muscular physique and tanned skin. His hair was shaved thin and he had a thin beard around his jaw line.

"Kelvin's a sweetheart. I'll get him to take a picture with you, if you want," Summer replied, allowing the husband comment to go unnoticed.

"Oh, that would be wonderful!"

"Come on." Summer grinned, grabbing his hand and pulling him away.

"Is the story in the rag true?" Harris asked, watching them walk away.

Brandt shook her head no.

"That's too bad. She's beautiful and seems really genuine, but after what you went through earlier this year, I wouldn't blame you for staying the hell away from women."

Brandt laughed. Harris and his wife had been guests at her wedding, along with Bernie and his husband.

~

When the party finally ended, Brandt took her suit jacket off and rolled her sleeves back before putting away the food that was salvageable and tossing the rest of it into the trash. Then she threw away all of the stray drink cups and beer bottles she found around the house and on the pool deck. When she walked back inside, Summer was leaning with her hip against the back of the couch.

"I thought you'd left," Brandt said, walking past her with the trash bag.

"I made it look like I left with Lewis, but I snuck back when everyone was gone."

Brandt nodded as she gathered all of the garbage bags and walked into the garage to place them in the proper receptacle.

"Are you mad at me?" Summer asked, following her.

"No," Brandt sighed, walking back inside to wash her hands. "Are you staying over?"

"Do you want me to?"

Brandt sat on a stool at the kitchen island and motioned for Summer, who stepped closer placing her arms around Brandt's neck. Brandt spread her legs and pulled Summer between them as she wrapped her arms loosely around her waist.

"I love you and I'll never tell you I don't want you to stay over, but I hope our relationship is more than simply spending the night together. I miss meeting you

170

for lunch and going out for dinner. How long are you planning on hiding yourself from the world?"

"I don't know," Summer sighed, sinking into her. "I love you and you're so much more than just sex to me. I'm sorry if I've made you feel that way."

"You haven't, but I don't want it to get to that either."

"Is this why you wanted me to meet that gay producer?"

"Bernie? Yes and no. I wanted you to see someone on the straight side of movies that is happily out and proud, but he's also a friend of mine."

Summer nodded. "Your friend, Bean, seems nice. She's not at all what I expected."

"Bean...well, she's just Bean. That's the best way to describe her. She's a movie nerd, which is why she's so good at what she does."

"Is she a lesbian too?"

"Yes, most of our employees are gay or lesbian, but a lot of the set people we contract hire for each movie are straight."

"Does she know about us?"

"No, but she knows how I know you, so she's familiar with our story. It won't take her long to figure it out. Bean and I have known each other a long time. There's not much we are able to slide past one another these days. I hate keeping this from her. She's my best friend and the closest thing to a sibling I'll ever have."

"I'm sorry."

Brandt ran her hands up and down Summer's back. "I know this isn't easy for you. Having your life in the spotlight sucks sometimes."

Chapter 24

Over the next two months, Brandt, Viv, and Bean had worked hard to finish the film editing and marketing to get it ready for the upcoming screening. Plus, the latest movie they'd released was up for an indie film award, so Brandt and Bean were preparing to attend that event in New York City. Brandt had thrown herself diligently into trying to finish her new script. Anything to keep her mind off Summer and the pictures of her and Lewis in the occasional tabloid.

Anyone Can Dance had sent it's pro dancers on a ten-city tour around the country, to perform routines for sold out crowds. Summer had worked hard choreographing a third of the routines before the tour had even started, so they'd barely seen each other in the month leading up to it, and she'd only seen her once since it had started. However, Lewis had been seen with her in at least three of the cities, which only made Brandt more pissed at the entire situation. Getting involved with someone in the closet was by far the most difficult thing she'd ever done and she was doing everything she could to be patient and understanding for Summer, but she had to draw the line at some point.

When the tour ended, there was a month before the new season of the show would start with completely new average dance partners for all of the pros. Summer had two weeks before she would meet her partner and begin rehearsing for the new season and she was beyond excited. This show had opened so many doors for her and given her a number of opportunities in only six months.

~

Brandt was in her home office working on her script when her phone rang. She smiled when she saw Summer's face on the caller ID.

"Hey," she answered.

"I miss you," Summer sighed.

"I miss you too."

"I wish I was going with you to the award show this weekend."

"Me too. Bean doesn't make a good date."

Summer laughed. "I promise to be at the next one with you."

"As my date?" Brandt asked.

"Maybe."

"Won't that get in the way of things with Lewis? You two are becoming quite the couple. I loved the selfie picture you posted of the two of you kissing in front of the water fountain."

"I didn't know you were on Twitter."

"I'm not," Brandt growled. "It was in the latest news regarding *Anyone Can Dance*, so I saw it."

"I'm sorry. It doesn't mean anything. You know that."

"I don't know if I do anymore. You tell me you love me, but you're gallivanting around town with this guy, kissing him and doing God only knows what else."

"I'm not sleeping with him, Brandt. He knows this is only for appearances."

"Fine. I believe you. I need to go pack and get some sleep."

"I love you. Have a safe flight and I hope you win the award. You deserve it."

"Thanks. Love you too." Brandt slammed her phone on the desk and went into her bedroom to pack her bag for the weekend.

~

The next day, after a long flight with a layover, Bean and Brandt arrived at the Waldorf Astoria Hotel where the awards were being presented in the ballroom that evening at a dinner gala. They quickly checked in and went to the hotel restaurant for dinner before heading up to their rooms to get cleaned up and ready for the private pre-party in the lobby bar that was being held for award nominees only.

Brandt texted Summer to let her know she'd arrived safely, then she took a long, hot shower. When she got out, she threw a little bit of gel into her short, messy blonde hair, then pulled on the black pants, shiny black shoes, and white wingtip collared shirt from her tux. She'd just finished her shirt studs and was working on the cufflinks when she heard a knock at the door.

"What's up?" she said, pulling it open as Bean rushed inside wearing a black, slim-fitting, sequin gown.

"I can't get this God damn dress zipped up!" Bean exclaimed.

Brandt laughed. Her best friend had always worn pants paired with a jacket at work and on set, but Bean always seemed to find her feminine side when they had to dress up for awards shows. She was one of those lesbians that wore pantsuits, but she preferred a dress over a tie any day.

"Well, are you going to help me or am I going to have to go find the maid?" Bean snapped.

"Alright, calm down and be still." Brandt tried to pull the zipper up, but it was stuck, so she pulled it back first, then tugged it all the way to the spot below her shoulder blades where the back of the dress stopped.

Bean spun around, checking herself out in the large mirror. "What do you think?"

"It's pretty."

"Why aren't you dressed? The pre-party starts in ten minutes."

Brandt rolled her eyes as she put her wine-colored satin vest on, buttoning the three buttons. Then, she tied the matching bowtie around her neck and pulled her jacket on. She finished the ensemble with a wine-colored pocket square and turned around to face Bean.

"Sexy as always. I don't know why you choose to stay single. Beautiful women turn their heads in your direction all the time. It's been eight months. I think it's time for you to put it behind you, my friend," Bean stated while straightening her bowtie.

Brandt smiled and shook her head. "What about you and Misty?"

"What about us? I might not flaunt my relationship, but I'm getting laid. You, on the other hand, obviously aren't. Your grouchy attitude lately is proof that it's time to get back in the saddle—literally."

Brandt laughed. "Come on before they run out of booze."

~

Bean and Brandt were standing in the bar, sipping champagne, when a commercial for the new season of *Anyone Can Dance* played on the nearby flat screen TV. Brandt's eyes were glued to it as they showed each of the pros paired together for two seconds each of a sultry dance while it announced the upcoming premiere date and time. Summer was paired with Kelvin and dressed in a two-piece top and fringed mini skirt that left little to the imagination, while he was shirtless. Brandt shook her head.

"Fancy meeting you here," a young woman said, sliding up next to Brandt and Bean. Kendra Milne was the lead actress from their film that was up for the award.

"Hey!" Bean exclaimed.

"Shall we?" Brandt said, nodding towards the doors to the ballroom that were opening slowly.

Bean and Kendra linked their arms through Brandt's as they made their way to the table they were all assigned to. They made small talk about the film and other things while everyone settled down at the large round tables throughout the room.

"We're seated in the back, so that means we probably didn't win," Bean teased.

Brandt laughed and turned in her chair to see the stage as the lights dimmed and the show began. One of the most well known lesbians in the entertainment industry hosted the show as different actors, actresses, and musicians presented each of the awards.

When they finally got to the Outstanding Film-Limited Release category, Bean squeezed Brandt's hand on the top of the table and Brandt held her breath. They listed each of the films and then opened the envelope, calling out the name of Brandt and Bean's film along with their names. All three women cheered and hugged each other before standing and walking towards the stage together.

"This isn't our first win, but each one has a special place in my heart, just as each of the movies that I've written." Brandt said, looking at the platinum and crystal award, before handing it to Bean. "There are so many people to thank. First, we have Kendra Milne, the amazing lead actress who is up here with us now, and the rest of the cast and crew, who worked their butts off filming in the freezing cold."

"We also have everyone back in L.A. who helped turn the film into a movie—Viv Winslow, Marshall Meeks, and everyone else at B2 Pictures. This is for all of us," Bean said, holding the award up. "But, we wouldn't be here if it wasn't for the creative mind of this woman right here." She smiled at Brandt.

They walked back stage to take the proverbial photographs with the awards association before going back to their seats for the remainder of the show.

~

Two hours later, the show finally ended and everyone dispersed. Brandt went to her room and left Summer a voicemail after she didn't answer the call. Then, she took off her jacket and undid her cufflinks, before rolling her sleeves back.

Fifteen minutes later, there was knock on her door. Brandt untied her tie, leaving it hanging down as she walked over, pulling it open.

"I come bearing gifts," Bean announced, holding up the bottle of wine in her hand. She was still in her dress, but her stocking feet were bare.

"In that case, come in," Brandt laughed.

"What were you doing?" Bean asked when she walked inside, noticing the TV was off and there weren't many lights on. She knew something had been bothering her best friend. Brandt had been on edge for the past few weeks and working extremely long hours. So, Bean had decided to get to the bottom of it before they headed home the next day.

"Not much of anything," Brandt answered honestly.

Bean opened the bottle of wine and poured it into the two glasses beside the ice bucket. Handing one to Brandt, she grabbed the other glass and sat down on the couch with her.

"What's going on with you?" she asked, sipping a generous amount of the chardonnay.

"What do you mean?" Brandt asked, stifling a yawn as she took a long drink from her glass.

"Something's been bothering you for a while now. I've let it go, but it's starting to affect your work. We're best friends. You can talk to me about anything, you know that."

Brandt leaned her head against the back of the couch and sighed. "It's complicated."

"Okay, well, un-complicate it then. Are you in some kind of trouble?"

"You have no idea." Brandt shook her head and swallowed the rest of her wine in one sip.

Bean poured her another round and listened as Brandt spent the next twenty minutes telling her secret. She couldn't believe what she was hearing. She was flabbergasted and definitely surprised that she'd had no idea what was going on.

"So, you've been together since the cruise?" Bean asked, still slightly shocked.

"No. We did have a great time and slept together on the cruise, but I thought it was over when she didn't return my call. We actually started dating about three weeks later when we saw each other again."

"And you've been together, in a relationship, this entire time? While she pretends to be straight."

"Yes."

"Brandt, this is crazy."

"I know."

"You're in over your head, aren't you?" Bean asked.

Brandt looked at her best friend's eyes. "I swore I'd never let another woman lead me around after what Jenna did," she sighed.

"I can certainly see the attraction. Summer's beautiful and if what she does on stage is any indication..." Bean grinned. "She also seems really sweet, but this isn't right, Brandt. You deserve so much more than hiding your relationship and pretending to be friends because she's in the closet. It's the twenty-first fucking century. It's not like she's going to be beheaded or stoned to death."

"She's scared it will ruin her career."

"Well, that's a chance she needs to take. Living a lie is going to catch up with her eventually."

"I know. It felt good to finally tell you. I'm sorry for keeping it from you, I just…I don't know what the hell to do."

"I think the first thing that needs to happen is getting rid of the fake boyfriend. That's absurd. Then, you really need to discuss your future together—if in fact, you want a future with her. If she loves you, she'll understand where you're coming from," Bean stated, pouring the last of the wine into their glasses.

"I agreed to the secrecy, so I'm going to sound like an asshole telling her I can't do it anymore," Brandt sighed.

"True, but you're hurting yourself by living this double life full of lies. I watched Jenna destroy everything you'd built together and I'm not going to let someone else do that to you."

Brandt stared down at the phone on the table in front of her. It still hadn't rang, meaning Summer either hadn't received her voicemail, or she was too busy to call her back.

"Do you love her?" Bean asked.

"More than I've ever loved anything in this world." Brandt chewed her lower lip and rolled her head to meet her best friend's eyes. "I loved Jenna, but it was nothing like the way I feel about Summer and that scares me a little."

Bean smiled. "Talk to her and lay it all out there. If she loves you as much as you love her, then she'll listen to what you're saying and understand why you're saying it." She grabbed Brandt's hand. "If she doesn't then you'll have to let her go. As much as it pains me to say that, knowing it will break your heart, it's the truth, hon. Some things are meant to be and some aren't."

~

Brandt arrived home the next afternoon and Summer rushed over to see her and give her congratulations in person. Brandt opened the door, welcoming the warmth of Summer in her arms, possibly for the last time, knowing what she had to do.

"I'm so proud of you. I wish I could've been there," Summer gushed.

"Thank you." Brandt grabbed her hand and walked over to the couch, where they sat down next to each other. "We need to talk about something."

"Okay? What's wrong?" Summer asked.

Brandt looked into her pale green eyes and felt a burning pang deep inside. "I can't do this anymore," she said.

"Do what?"

"Lewis, the lying, all of it. You're either all in with this relationship or I'm out."

"Are you serious?"

"Summer, I love you," she sighed. "More than I've ever loved anyone, but I can't keep going like this. I'm sorry. I'm done chasing something that may not have been there to start with."

"What's that supposed to mean?" Summer huffed as a few tears escaped her eyes.

"If you love me as much as I love you, then you know how wrong it is to lie and pretend to date other people while we sneak around to be together." Brandt shook her head. "I spent three years chasing after my relationship with Jenna, fighting to stay ahead, and in the end, it was a complete waste of time and I got hurt."

"I'm not your ex-girlfriend."

"I know that, Summer, but I'm done lying to everyone, my friends, family, co-workers, whomever, and I'm done watching you parade around with Lewis like you're in love with him. I want the girl I met on the cruise, the one who had fun with me and was happy to be with me. Whoever you are right now, I don't know you."

Summer wiped her years. "I can't just come out to the world, Brandt. I'll lose everything!"

"You might not lose anything, but if we don't stop all of these lies, you're going to lose me."

Brandt moved to grab her hand and Summer stood up, walking away from the couch.

"Summer?" Brandt murmured as she watched her leave without looking back. When the door closed, she broke down, crying for the pain she caused herself and Summer, crying for the hatred she had towards the situation, and crying for the extreme loss she felt as a hole tore open her heart. "Damn it!" she screamed.

Chapter 25

Brandt spent the next few days avoiding anything that reminded her of Summer, including the entertainment news and the TV, as well as the coffee shop and restaurants near her office. When she walked into the building on Wednesday, there was a hot cup of coffee, just the way she liked it, sitting on her desk. Brandt pursed her lips and sunk down into her chair, drinking a long sip. Stopping her morning trips to the café made her body miss the caffeine buzz that usually started her day.

"You can thank me later," Bean said, bursting into the room, nearly causing Brandt to spill the coffee she was slowly enjoying all over herself. "We have bigger things to deal with right now," she continued, tossing a letter onto Brandt's desk.

"What's this?"

"Deana Pollack, the actress that is playing Paola in Francesca's film, our next picture, has decided she wants twice the money offered in her contract. Apparently, because we're winning awards, we can afford to pay more. This is the letter from her agent."

Brandt picked up the paper, reading the couple of paragraphs and shaking her head. "We're more of a micro-budget company than low-budget to begin with, so she should be happy with what we'd offered!"

"My thoughts exactly!" Bean flopped down in the chair across from Brandt's desk. "What are we going to do?"

"Release her."

"What?"

"I'm serious. Void her contract and move on with someone else."

"We'd have to start the casting process all over again. Fran really likes her."

"Fran's not producing this movie, we are. Now, release her from her contract effective immediately. Maybe this will teach her not to play games and to avoid shady, two-bit agents who can't find their ass from a hole in the wall in the future."

Bean raised her eyebrows.

"It's not like we're filming right now. We have a couple of months, so that's plenty of time to replace her."

"Alright, but you're telling Fran."

"Fine." Brandt shrugged.

"You have more balls than I do," Bean said, shaking her head as she stood up.

"I hope that was a compliment!" Brandt called to her back as Bean left the room.

~

That evening, Brandt walked into her house, exhausted from dealing with the fallout from firing the actress from the upcoming picture. She'd just changed into her swimsuit and was headed outside to swim some laps when there was a loud knock on her front door. She tossed the towel over her shoulder and walked over, peering through the peephole. Surprised, she pulled the door open to reveal Summer standing in front of her wearing a pair of cut-off jean shorts, a black halter-style tank top that hugged her body, and flip flops. Her hair was up in a loose bun.

"Can we talk?" Summer asked softly.

"Sure. I was just about to go swimming. Would you like to join me?" Brandt asked.

Summer furrowed her brow in confusion. That's not at all what she'd been expecting. "Are you sure?" she asked.

"You want to talk and I want to go swimming," Brandt shrugged closing the door behind her. "Kill two birds with one stone."

"I don't have a swimsuit," Summer said.

"That never stopped you before." Brandt headed through the French doors to the pool deck.

She set her towel on the chaise lounge and dove head-first into the deep end, swimming halfway across the pool before coming up for air. She turned around in time to see the delicate splash from Summer's dive and waited for the younger woman to break the surface nearby. The sun was going down behind the mountain in the distance and she hadn't bothered turning the pool light on, so she could barely see the naked body under the water in front of her.

Summer looked up at the orange and red colors painting the sky, before turning her eyes to the women a couple feet away. "I knew the day I spilled my coffee on you that I wanted to see you again. When I crashed into your car at the light, I couldn't get you out of my head.

Seeing you on the cruise made my heart skip a beat, and the first time we slept together, I fell in love with you."

Brandt held her ground as Summer moved a little closer.

"I'm sorry. I should've seen you for who you are and our relationship for what it was, not what I was scared of everything becoming. I made one huge mistake after the other and I pulled you into the closet with me," Summer sighed. "I love you more than I've ever loved anything or anyone and that scares me to death, Brandt. The connection between us is so powerful, I did everything I could to pull away and put distance there without even realizing it." Summer wiped the tears falling from her eyes. "Damn it," she hissed. "We're meant to be together, you and I. I know it in my heart and I feel it deep down inside. This is where I belong, with you, at your side—not trying to be a different person and pretending to be with someone else. I won't deny how much that terrifies me, but I trust you with all of my heart."

She moved closer, stopping less than a foot away. "You once told me you weren't going to chase me. I'm giving myself to you, Brandt. All in. No games, no running." She swallowed hard as her heart pounded in her chest. "Tell me you don't love me like I love you, and I'll leave and never look back."

Brandt's heart leapt into her throat when she tried to speak. She slowed her racing mind and simply looked at the woman in front of her, seeing the reason she knew she'd see her once again after the coffee shop incident, the reason she had to get away from the accident scene so fast and the reason she couldn't go the entire cruise without getting to know her. The attraction between them was the strongest thing she'd ever felt in her life and she knew above everything else that this connection was real.

"I love you so damn much it hurts," Brandt murmured, closing the distance between them as Summer wrapped her arms around her neck.

Their lips met in a slow, passionate kiss that left them both panting and wanting more. Brandt ran her hands up and down the silky, wet skin of Summer's naked back as their bodies pressed together. She walked backwards until Summer's back was nearly against the wall. Then, she cupped her ass, lifting Summer out of the water and onto the edge of the pool.

Summer arched her back, bending her knees as she put her legs over Brandt's shoulders when she moved closer. Brandt pressed her crotch against the pool jet and bent down, putting her mouth where Summer wanted it, while the jet messaged her clit like a vibrator.

Summer's wet body glistened in the moonlight like a goddess as Brandt licked a steady pattern while rubbing her crotch around the jet massaging her below the water. Summer's panting and occasional cries of pleasure brought Brandt closer and closer to her own release. Brandt lost control when Summer let out a guttural sound and held Brandt's head down. She licked and sucked Summer's clit while pressing herself against the jet pulsing around her crotch. They moaned together, climaxing simultaneously.

They both stilled and Brandt finally caught her breath, climbing out of the pool on shaky legs. Summer was lying flat on her back on the pool deck, looking up at the stars when Brandt smiled, holding her hand out to her.

"I think I'm dead and this is heaven," Summer murmured, taking the offered hand and letting Brandt pull her to her feet.

"I could spend eternity looking at your naked body." Brandt grinned.

Summer laughed and kissed her softly. "I love you," she whispered, pulling back enough to look into Brandt's eyes.

"I don't think I'll ever tire of hearing you say that." Brandt wrapped her arms around Summer, pulling her closer. "I love you too," she murmured against her. "More than I've ever loved anything," she added.

~

The next morning, Brandt stretched like a Cheshire cat in the cool sheets. She opened her eyes to see Summer leaning against the French doors, looking out at the mountain peak in the distance. Realizing Brandt was awake, Summer turned and walked back over to the bed, where she stood next to the side Brandt was lying on.

"Good morning," Brandt yawned, sitting up.

"Yes, it is." Summer smiled, kissing her cheek.

"You look like the cat that ate the canary. What's up?" Brandt arched her brow.

"I'm going to tell the other dancers about me."

"Really?"

"Yeah. The show is about to start back up and I'm tired of lying."

"That's a huge step." Brandt smiled. "I think it's great."

Summer ran her hand through Brandt's short, messy hair. "I also called Lewis and broke off the fake relationship," she said.

"Wow."

"I'm not going to fly out of the closet or anything like that, but I'm not going to lie to cover up who I am. Not anymore."

Brandt reached up, pulling Summer down into her lap. Summer laughed, wrapping her arms around Brandt's neck.

"Move in with me," Brandt murmured, looking into her beautiful eyes. She'd never said those words to anyone, not even the woman she'd planned to marry and spend the rest of her life with. It both scared and excited her.

"Are you serious?" Summer leaned back, gauging the expression on Brandt's face.

"Yes. If I wasn't, I wouldn't have asked."

"I...uh," Summer faltered, trying to put words together.

"I know I live further away from the studio and everything, but—"

"That's not..." Summer shook her head, stopping her. Smiling brightly, she said, "I don't care where you live, I want to be with you."

"So, is that a yes?" Brandt asked.

Summer grinned and kissed her lips softly. "Yes," she whispered, pushing her back on the bed.

Chapter 26

Over the next two weeks, Brandt and Bean screened the new movie and Summer found someone to sublet her apartment, allowing her to move in quickly. She'd left most of furniture behind for the girl who was leasing her place, so she hadn't had to bring a lot with her, but Brandt still made room to accommodate Summer's belongings. She even moved her clothes around to give her half of the space in the large, walk-in closet in the master bedroom.

Their first weekend living together was unlike anything Brandt had expected. They'd cooked together, cleaned the house, and watched TV like a regular couple. Summer was still leery about public appearances, and Brandt completely understood. She'd already taken a few huge steps as it was, so Brandt had done all of the grocery shopping.

~

When Monday rolled around, Summer headed to the studio to meet her new dance partner, while Brandt went to the office as usual after they had coffee together that morning at the café they frequented, of course.

"You look chipper. I take it the weekend went well?" Bean sat down in the seat across from Brandt at her desk.

"Yeah." Brandt nodded. "I haven't lived with anyone since I was a freshman in college, and even then I hated it, but this is completely different."

"I doubt you were sleeping with your college roommate," Bean laughed.

Brandt raised an eyebrow and Bean gasped.

"I'm kidding. I've actually never lived with anyone I dated—well, until now."

"I'm glad you worked things out. I don't think I've ever seen you this happy."

"The way I felt about Jenna is nothing compared to this. She literally takes my breath away, Bean."

"I still can't believe this is the same girl who spilled coffee on you and rear-ended your car." She shook her head. "I thought you would knock that woman's head off if you ever saw her again and instead, you slept with her and fell in love," she laughed.

"Yeah." Brandt smiled.

Bean silently hoped Summer didn't break her best friend's heart. She strongly believed in karma and things happening for a reason, which made her think they were meant to be together, since everything that pulled them apart ended up pushing them even closer.

"You look lost in thought," Brandt said.

Bean grinned. "I was just thinking about the rest of this month. We need to go back to Vancouver and lock down our location for Francesca's film. We're scheduled to start shooting in a few months."

"I know." Brandt looked at the calendar on her computer. "I have time in three weeks."

"I want to film some of it in the studio, so we'll need Greg with us from set design."

"That's fine. See if those dates are fine with him and have Renee book everything."

~

Brandt pulled into the garage attached to her house and was surprised to see Summer's SUV parked inside. She wondered how long it was going to take her to get used to the fact that they were living together.

"I thought I heard you come in," Summer said, peering down from the top of the stairs.

Brandt smiled and made her way up, stopping to kiss her softly before setting her briefcase in her office and going into their bedroom.

"How was your day?" Brandt asked.

"Hectic."

"What did the dancers say?"

Summer sat on the bench at the foot of the bed. "It was crazy in the studio today, but I did find time to talk to India, Kelvin, and Pierre since we're doing a pair dance together for the opening of the show."

"Well?" Brandt waited.

"They couldn't be happier for me, and of course, the first thing they asked was if you and I were together." She smiled.

"What did you say?" Brandt asked, walking into the closet to change out of her pantsuit.

"I told them I was head-over-heels in love and we were living together. It felt so liberating, but they also agreed to keep things quiet. Pierre is gay and said he had some issues with one of the producers when he was first cast."

"That's such bullshit." Brandt shook her head.

"I know, but it felt good to at least tell them. I'm not as close to the other dancers, so I don't know if I'll tell them anytime soon."

"It's your choice who you tell, and how, and when you tell them. I'll stand by whatever you do. How's the new partner, by the way?"

"Robert Holmes is his name. He goes by Rob and he's a business owner from Texas. He's actually not a bad dancer, probably because he's been line dancing and two-stepping since he was a kid," she said, neglecting to tell her how much of an asshole he was.

Brandt laughed, poking her head out of the closet. "Is that a good thing?"

Summer shrugged. "Any dance skills are better than none."

"That makes sense."

"What about you? How was your day?" Summer asked as Brandt walked out of the closet wearing a pair of shorts and a t-shirt.

"It was fine. We fired the lead actress for our new film after she tried to shaft us on her contract a few weeks ago, so Bean's been running like crazy to get her replaced. We're going up to Vancouver for three days next week to work on the location for the new film and go over the set design. We'll be working in the studio we use up there, as well as doing a little bit of on-site shooting at the location."

"That sounds like fun," Summer said, wrapping her arms loosely around Brandt's waist.

"Not really. Bean's extremely particular and sometimes she drives me nuts, but she's a hell of a director, so I trust her instincts." Brandt kissed her softly. "I like this living together thing." She grinned.

"Me too. It certainly has its perks," Summer murmured, kissing her back.

"I know you don't want to go out for dinner."

"No, not really. We started the press stuff for the show last week, so the buzz is back in everyone's head. I'm not really in the mood for paparazzi."

"Yeah, me either. How about stir-fry and salad?"

"That sounds divine," Summer replied, lacing her fingers with Brandt's as they walked downstairs to the kitchen to prepare their dinner together.

~

Summer worked diligently over the next week and a half, trying to teach Rob how to do the waltz, which was the dance for the first night of the show. He picked up the moves easier than she'd expected, which made her think she may have a shot at winning this season, and by the time Wednesday night rolled around, they were more than ready for the first show of the season.

Brandt sat in the second row of the audience, watching the performance as each of the pros, paired with their average partner, took the stage one at a time to perform their personally choreographed waltz to the song they'd chosen. She couldn't help clapping a little louder when Summer stepped onto the floor. She was wearing a beautiful, champagne colored chiffon gown with sparkly sequins from the waist up and see-thru lace sleeves. The sides of the dress were cutout, showing off her impeccable upper body. Rob had short thinning brown hair with a matching mustache and goatee. He was wearing a dark gray suit with a champagne colored necktie and seemed extremely confident as he lead Summer around, gliding gracefully across the dance floor. When the song ended, he dipped her in a move that would've made Humphrey Bogart proud.

Brandt couldn't help feeling a pang of jealousy. She wasn't much of a dancer and would probably never lead Summer in a beautiful dance like the one she'd just witnessed. Nevertheless, it was a beautiful sight to watch when Summer was dancing.

The pro dancers came out in pairs and also in groups between the other dances, showing off major skills as they completed multiple routines—some of which were Latin dances that required very little clothing. Brandt had always found it sexy when Summer performed the sultry moves of the spicy dances, but she also cringed wondering how the little bit of fabric stayed in place.

After the last pair, the full troupe came out for two big routines and then they broke for a commercial to tally the online, text message, and called-in votes, before revealing the pair ranking for the evening. Summer and Rob were at the top of the leader board with the highest votes and would dance last next week.

Once it was over, Brandt went backstage where Pierre, Kelvin, and India all came up to her to say hello. Summer smiled brightly when she saw her.

"Hey! How did you like the show?" Summer beamed.

"It was great. You danced beautifully, as usual."

"Brandt, this is my dance partner, Rob."

Brandt nodded and shook his hand as he eyed her up and down.

"Do you work on the show?" he asked.

"No. She's a screenwriter and a movie producer," Summer said.

He simply nodded and went to go change clothes.

"He's not very talkative," Brandt murmured.

"Some of the average people are overwhelmed at first by the people and cameras. They get used to it after a few weeks."

"I hate that I'm going to miss it next week. After missing a lot of last season while filming of my movie, I was hoping to be here to support you every week," Brandt proclaimed.

"Aww, you're sweet. I'm going to miss you either way. It'll be lonely in the house without you for a week."

"I know, but it'll go by sooner than you think."

"Hey, would you two like to go out with us?" Pierre asked, stepping up to them. "We're going to grab some dinner."

Summer looked at Brandt, who shrugged, letting her know it was her choice.

"Brandt's going out of town all next week, so I kind of want to spend some time with her before that," Summer replied.

"Sounds good. Maybe another time. I'll see you tomorrow, bright and early." He smiled before hugging her goodbye. "You killed it tonight, by the way."

"Thanks." Summer smiled.

Chapter 27

Brandt and Bean had been to Vancouver hundreds of times since they'd owned their production company, but every time they started a new movie, it was like being there for the first time. Bean had to look at every single place on her list and then some before making a decision on where to shoot the movie. When it was one of Brandt's movies, they often had to compromise on a location instead of trying to force each other to see eye-to-eye on their vision.

"I still like that hotel downtown," Bean sighed.

Brandt rolled her head against the airplane seat from the window to the woman sitting next to her.

"We decided to shoot those scenes in the studio," Brandt replied.

"I know. I really like the park. I think those scenes will be great, but—"

"We decided on using the studio and not the hotel that wanted to charge all of our arms and legs for two days of filming."

"I know, but we still have to build the set."

"Bean, we have a long plane ride," Brandt warned, hoping she'd drop it. Their budget for the film was low and she'd planned to keep it that way.

"Fine," Bean huffed as she opened the entertainment magazine she'd picked up in the airport. "Look at this," she said, showing Brandt the picture of Summer dancing on the show. "She really is stunning."

"You should see her dance in person. I'll see if she can get an extra ticket for one of the shows and you can go with me."

"That sounds like fun. How did she do this week?"

"The dance for the week was Jive and her partner was actually really good at it, so they're still at the top of leader board."

"That's great."

~

Brandt was glad to be home after a long week, but Summer had spent most of the weekend in the studio. Their dance for the upcoming week was cha-cha, the first Latin dance of the season, and Rob was having a difficult time getting his hips to move. So, Summer spent a lot of extra time working with him while Brandt hung around the house, working on one of the older scripts she was trying to finish. Neither Summer nor Brandt wanted to see Monday roll around, but it came and went before they even realized it.

The next day, Brandt had just returned from having lunch with Summer at their favorite sushi place, that allowed them to enter and exit through the back door. She stepped into her office building and smelled the scent of a familiar perfume. Her eyebrows drew together in question as she walked around to the small lobby upfront.

"Having a late lunch?" Jenna asked.

Brandt nodded. She hadn't spoken to her ex since the night before their supposed wedding. She'd hadn't really thought about what she'd say to her if and when she saw her again because she'd never planned to.

"What do you want?"

"Can we talk?" Jenna asked, standing up. She was wearing an ivory colored short skirt with a black blouse that haltered around her neck. Her long blonde hair hung down her back.

"Fine, but I don't have a lot of time." Brandt walked towards her office with Jenna behind her. She wasn't sure why she wanted to hear what she had to say, but she felt like she was owed an explanation either way.

Bean turned the corner in time to see them enter Brandt's office and shut the door. She gasped in shock and hurried up to Renee's desk.

"When did Jenna Harte get here?"

"About a half hour ago. I told her Brandt was out to lunch, but she insisted on waiting to see her. I thought she was history."

"She is," Bean stated as she walked away.

~

Brandt sat down behind her desk and Jenna sat in one of the chairs across from her.

"I'm sorry, Brandt. I never meant to run away. I'm back now."

"Excuse me?" Brandt huffed. "You ran out on me on our wedding day." Brandt shook her head. "How's the wedding planner, by the way?"

"I'm sorry. I was overwhelmed with the wedding planning and it scared me. You were always gone and I

199

turned to her. We hooked up a couple of times and she convinced me that being with her in New York was better for me. I hurt you and I'm sorry."

"Are you kidding me with this? Jenna, you fucked our wedding planner multiple times and ran off with her on our wedding day. What are you doing here in my office?"

"I know you're upset, but I realized that wasn't where I wanted to be. I'm home now."

Brandt laughed. "Am I supposed to welcome you back to California?"

"I said I was sorry. Can't you forgive me?"

"Forgive you? Jenna, you have no idea what you put me through. Then, on top of everything, you left me with the bill! You're a selfish asshole, Jenna—plain and simple. I have no room for you in my life."

"I still love you, Brandt. I know I hurt you. I made a huge mistake, but we can work this out."

"There's nothing to work out. I gave you three years of my life and you dumped me off like trash on the side of the road and never looked back." Brandt shook her head. "I want my three years back since they were obviously a waste."

"Our three years together were wonderful," Jenna said.

"If everything was so perfect, why do it?"

"I told you, I needed some time to find myself. I was in over my head with everything and you were never here."

"Why didn't you just talk to me, Jenna? Instead, you ran off with some whore. Speaking of, isn't the wedding planner wondering where you are?"

"Brandt, I never talked to you because I didn't know what to say. I didn't know who I was anymore. Anyway, it's over with Tiffany. I got it out of my system, so we can move forward, you and I."

"Oh, I definitely moved forward. In fact, I've been dating someone for a while now. We're living together, actually."

"What?"

"Yep."

"She's living in your house with you?" Jenna looked stunned.

"Yes and I'm happy, maybe for the first time in my life. Your letter said you needed to go find yourself—well, I took your advice."

"Who is she?"

"You don't know her."

Jenna sneered. "Is she the dancer on that show that I saw you with in the tabloids a few months ago?"

Brandt smiled. "Is that why you're here? You think I moved on with someone else and you're back to fuck up my life all over again." She shook her head. "I think this conversation is over. Go back to New York, Jenna. It suits you better than L.A.," she said, escorting her out of the building.

As soon as Brandt plopped down in her chair, Bean appeared in front of her.

"What the hell was that all about?"

"Holy shit!" Brandt opened her eyes and jumped an inch off her chair. "You need a damn bell around your neck or something," she chided.

"I'm not a cat!" Bean huffed. "So?" She raised her eyebrows.

"I thought I'd died and gone to hell when I walked in and saw her in the lobby," Brandt sighed.

"I bet. What did she want?"

"To get back together. Apparently, she's done finding herself."

"No way!"

"I'm serious." Brandt rubbed her temples.

"What did you say to her?"

"I said okay. I'm meeting her for dinner tonight."

"What!" Bean yelled. "Are you stupid?"

Brandt laughed. "That's what you get for sneaking up on me!"

"Ha-ha."

"I told her to go pound sand." Brandt shook her head. "I'm happy with Summer and even if I wasn't with her, there's no way in hell I'd get back with Jenna. I'd rather die a slow death from rat poisoning."

"I'll make a note of that."

"You do so, and if you catch me with her ever again, you have my permission to start administering it in lethal doses." She rubbed her head again. "God, that bitch makes me crazy. I can't believe she thought she could run off with the wedding planner, fuck her for eight or nine months, then walk back into my life like nothing happened!"

"I'm not even a part of it and I need a drink."

"Me too. Let's get out of here." Brandt stood up and grabbed her briefcase.

~

Brandt and Bean walked into Oliver's Martini Bar fifteen minutes later and grabbed a high top table.

"I can't believe we came here. I haven't been here since the night before my non-wedding," Brandt said, ordering a specialty, fruity martini from the menu.

"Yeah, but they have the best drinks."

"Says the boring, dry martini drinker." Brandt shook her head. "Have you ever tried anything else here?"

"Nope."

"Come on, live a little."

"Fine," Bean growled and waved the waitress back over. "Can you change my drink to a..." She looked at the menu with at least fifty martinis listed. "Chocolate Dream, please?"

The woman nodded and smiled as she walked away.

"See, are you happy?"

"Hell yeah, because that one is good, so I'll drink it if you don't."

Bean shook her head and pushed her glasses up.

"Are you going to tell Summer about today?"

"Of course. Isn't that what you do in a relationship? Tell each other everything? It's one of the main things that came between Jenna and me to begin with. She never talked to me about things."

"I still can't believe she's back in town. Is she planning on staying?"

"I have no idea. She's obviously living in a fairytale if she thought we'd pick right back up where we left off. She needs to move out to Anaheim with the characters of Disneyland."

"Did she say why she left?"

"No. Well, she did mention being scared and overwhelmed with the wedding and I was gone, so she screwed the wedding planner or something to that effect."

"Nice," Bean laughed. "Why did she return?"

"She's home so we can be together again."

"That makes no sense."

"I know, which is why I finally got the truth out of her. Jenna saw a tabloid with me and Summer in it. She wanted to know if it was true."

"What did you say?"

"I didn't tell her who it was, but I said I was in love and she was living with me in my house. Bean, you should've seen her face. It was like our three years together flashed before her beady eyes and never once did I ask her to move in. It wasn't until we were engaged that it was even mentioned."

"I bet that stung a little bit." Bean tried to hide her smile.

"I don't care. It did a lot more than fucking sting when she ran out and left me with all of our wedding guests and oh, the $100,000 bill that went with it for the wedding of her dreams that she just had to have!"

Bean laughed.

"I need a vacation," Brandt sighed.

"Me too."

~

After two martinis, Brandt headed home to relax after a disastrous afternoon. She was sitting in the hot tub with her arms along the top edge and her head back on a folded towel, relaxing with her eyes closed, when Summer walked in from a long day of rehearsal.

"Oh, that looks comfortable," she cooed, stepping outside.

"It is," Brandt replied, squinting her eyes.

Summer quickly changed from her sports bra and baggy gym pants to a bright yellow string bikini that left little to the imagination. She hurried outside and stepped down into the hot, bubbly water, groaning loudly.

"How was the rest of your day?" she asked, straddling Brandt's lap and wrapping her arms around her neck.

"Jenna was in my office when I returned from lunch," Brandt sighed.

"Your ex?"

"That would be correct."

"I thought she took off to NYC?"

"She's back home, she said. Apparently thought we'd pick back up where we left off."

"What?"

Brandt wrapped her arms around the lithe, athletic body of the woman in her lap. "I told her I was madly in love and we were living together."

"Are you?"

"What?" Brandt looked into her eyes.

"Madly in love." Summer smiled.

"Would you like me to show you how much?" Brandt teased, sliding her hand between her and Summer to rub the front of Summer's bathing suit bottoms.

Summer moaned and bit her bottom lip before meeting Brandt's mouth in a searing kiss that left them both breathless.

"Why is it every time we come out here, one of us has clothes on?" Brandt chided.

Summer grinned sheepishly.

Brandt moved her other hand up Summer's back, untying her top and tossing it over her shoulder onto the deck behind her. Then, she worked her other hand under the bottoms that were obstructing her view of Summer's naked body as the sun began to set over the city around them.

Chapter 28

The following week, Brandt walked into the studio where Summer was rehearsing for the show carrying a beautiful flower arrangement to surprise her for her birthday. She stood to the side, watching as Summer moved through a few troubling steps of the choreography for her and Rob's Paso Doble routine. Summer was dressed in red and black, zebra-striped yoga pants with a red sports bra, black tank top, and black sneakers. Her wavy hair was up in a ponytail.

"Hey!" Summer squealed, running over when she saw Brandt leaning against the wall.

"I was in the neighborhood," Brandt said, smiling at her. "Happy birthday!"

"Thank you! Oh, my God, these are beautiful!" Summer took the vase, hugging Brandt quickly.

Brandt smiled as her eyes landed on Rob, who standing on the other side of the room dressed in sweatpants and sneakers. he was staring back at her with his arms crossed over his bare chest. She knew he didn't know about Summer, so she understood why she was distant.

"I need to get back to the office," Brandt murmured. "I'll see you later. I hope you have a great day."

"Thank you," Summer whispered, looking into her eyes. She'd wanted nothing more than to wrap her arms around Brandt and kiss her, but she still hadn't told anyone other than the couple of pro dancers with whom she was friends.

~

Brandt spent the afternoon going through a new stack of potential scripts with Bean. Brandt was working on a new one of her own, but they also liked to produce other screenwriter's stories that they both felt passionate about.

When her eyes felt like they were going to bug out of her head from reading one synopsis after another, she headed home for the day and picked up take-out from their favorite sushi restaurant on the way.

The food was on the table with a bottle of wine when summer arrived home a little bit later.

"Is that what I think it is?" Summer asked as she set her flowers on the island in the kitchen.

Brandt wrapped her arms around her from behind. "Yes."

"I'm all stinky from busting my ass in rehearsal today. Thank you for the flowers, by the way. They're beautiful." Summer leaned back with her head turned, kissing Brandt's lips softly.

"Don't worry about showering, let's eat first," Brandt said, grabbing her hand and walking into the dining room.

They each drank a glass of wine as they quickly ate their dinner.

"I didn't realize how hungry I was," Summer exclaimed as she helped Brandt clear the table.

"How was the rest of your day?" Brandt asked while she removed the trash bag from the can under the sink to take it out.

"Fine. Rob is still struggling a little bit with one section of the dance, but I think he finally got it today. I stepped up the choreography because I know he can do it," Summer replied as she started washing the couple of dishes they'd used.

"I got the feeling he wasn't too thrilled when I surprised you today. What's his problem?"

"He's..." Summer turned to face her. "He's a homophobic bigot," she sighed.

"What? Are you serious?"

"Oh, yeah. He's constantly making racial slurs and sexist comments and he goes off on the rants about gays that make me want to kill him with my sneaker, but there's nothing I can do about it."

"Summer, you can tell the producer. This is crazy!"

"I'm still new. I don't need any issues. The season's almost over anyway."

"How could you go on for three weeks with this asshole and not tell me?"

"I knew you'd be upset, but it's my problem and I'm dealing with it. Brandt, I'm doing what I love, what I want to be doing. I'm not going to let this piece of shit stop me."

Brandt wrapped her arms around Summer, pulling her close. "I love you. You can tell me anything. I'm more disturbed that you kept it from me. I know you're a grown woman and you can handle yourself, but I hope that I'm a big enough part of your life that you'd want to tell me everything."

"I do, and I wanted to tell you so many times. I'm sorry."

"Does anyone else know?" Brandt wondered.

"Yeah, India."

"Are you okay with dealing with this asshole for the rest of the season?"

"Yes. I can handle him. What he doesn't know won't hurt him or me."

Brandt kissed her. "Come on, let's not let this ruin your birthday," she said, grabbing her hand and leading her up the stairs.

The garden tub in the master bathroom was full of hot water and bubbles with red rose petals and candles.

"I love you," Summer murmured.

Brandt smiled and shed her clothes before getting into the hot bath with her. Summer leaned her body back against Brandt's as the water and bubbles enclosed them up to her shoulders. Brandt ran her hands up her arms to her shoulders, massaging softly.

"That feels so good," Summer moaned as Brandt continued kneading the tense muscles of her back, then moved to her neck before slipping down to her breasts. "Those are sore from dancing," Summer laughed.

"Just checking." Brandt grinned.

~

Once the water became cooler, they climbed out and began toweling off. Summer walked into the bedroom to retrieve some clothes from her side of the dresser and stopped when she saw a purple gift bag on the bed.

"What's this?" she asked, walking over to it.

"Looks like a birthday gift to me." Brandt grinned.

"Brandt, the flowers and dinner were enough. You didn't have to get me a gift."

Brandt shrugged. "Maybe it's for me."

Summer laughed and pulled the tissue paper out. A square-shaped, black velvet box was leaning against the side. She lifted an eyebrow as she pulled it out. Brandt watched her face go from questioning to surprise when she flipped the box open, revealing a diamond pendant necklace and matching earrings.

"It's gorgeous!" Summer exclaimed, looking up at her. "Brandt!" She smiled, shaking her head.

"I guess that means you like it."

"I love it!" Summer set the box down and wrapped her arms around Brandt's neck, bringing their naked bodies together. "You don't have to buy me gifts," she whispered before kissing her passionately.

"I didn't buy them for you," Brandt teased. "I think you should wear them to bed...for me."

Summer raised an eyebrow.

"Only them," Brandt added.

"Oh, really?" Summer bit her bottom lip. "I think that can be arranged," she replied, kissing her again.

Chapter 29

Brandt took Bean with her to the fourth week of the show, where Summer and Rob had performed the amazing Paso routine she'd been working so hard on. Brandt had told Bean a little bit about Rob being a bigot, so neither of them had any words for him when they went backstage after the show.

"What did you think?" Summer beamed.

"It was amazing," Bean exclaimed. "You're even more incredible than Brandt described. I'm a huge fan of the show anyway, so thank you for inviting me."

"I'm glad you came," Summer replied, hugging her. "And you," she said, walking over to Brandt. "I know it was you who sent the mysterious red rose that was laying on my dressing station when I got here."

"What? Me?"

"The note gave you away!" Summer chided, wrapping her arms around her neck. Brandt threaded her arms around Summer's waist, pulling her close.

"I love you," Brandt whispered into her ear. She'd sent the mysterious flower to let her know she was the best dancer on that floor and no one was going to hold her back from doing what she loved. Brandt would make sure of that.

Summer pulled away, smiling at her and running her hand over Brandt's cheek. She turned around and re-introduced Bean to the pro dancers with whom she was friends. They'd met at the wrap party for the last season, but she wasn't sure if any of them had remembered.

Rob watched all of the exchanges from a few feet away before stepping closer. "You sure are around a lot," he sneered to Brandt. "If I didn't know any better, I'd think you were a dyke with rubber hard-on for Summer. Does she know you're a sick pervert?"

"Excuse me?" Brandt replied loudly.

"Brandt," Summer said, trying to hold her back. "It's okay, let it go."

"Wait, are you a dyke too? No fucking way!" He smiled. "Wait until I tell everyone all about your juicy little secret. I bet you won't have thousands of people falling all over you when they find out what you really are!"

Brandt lurched forward, jacking him against the wall with his shirt collar bunched in her hands. "I'll kick your ass you sexist, homophobic piece of shit!"

Kelvin had heard the end of Rob's sentence as he made his way over to them. Pierre was already trying to stop the mayhem when he stepped in, encouraging Brandt to release the jerk and let the producers handle it. Brandt finally shoved him to the side and stepped away. Pierre had already gone to get the producer who returned with him to the dressing area.

"Are all of your fucking dancers fags and dykes? Wait until America finds out what this show is really about!" Rob yelled.

"Whoa, calm down," the producer said. "First of all, sexual orientation is not something we discriminate

213

against. In fact, we don't care at all and neither does most of the world, so you're out on a very shaky tree limb at the moment with nothing under you but the ground. I suggest you cool off and take a look at your contract. You're under a confidentiality clause until this season of the show is over, so there's a reason to stop making threats. It's been a long couple of weeks and tempers are flaring as the competition heats up, so I'm going to let all of this go, but if I catch you making any more bigoted slurs towards anyone involved with this show, I'll void your contract and sue you for defamation of character and breech of contract. Meaning you'll owe us back anything and everything we've paid you so far, and then some. Are we clear?"

Rob nodded.

"Go back to your hotel and calm down. Have a drink, take a hot shower, whatever it is you need to do to relax."

Everyone watched Rob walk away.

"What if he makes good on his promise to out Summer and anyone else that's gay on the show?" Pierre said.

The producer pursed his lips. "We'll sue him for defamation, but that's about all we can do. He's a dickhead. I knew we were going to have a problem with him when I saw his interview tape, but the director liked him dancing in his video. We're a television show above anything else, so it's all about the ratings."

"What do you think will happen to the ratings after he goes on his rampage? Because you know he will," Brandt asked.

"We'll ride that wave when we get to it." He looked at the couple of pros standing around him. "You all did well tonight. The show was great and had the highest voting turnout that we've had all season."

Brandt and Summer watched him walk away.

"Well, that happened." Summer shook her head.

"Rob needs his ass kicked," India growled.

"It'll happen, especially if he does go on some kind of rant. He was a nobody before this show and he'll be a nobody afterwards too," Kelvin added, giving Summer a hug. "We all care about you and we'll stand behind you."

"Thanks, guys." Summer smiled.

"We're going to get out of here. I'll see you at home," Brandt sighed, kissing Summer's cheek before leaving with Bean.

Summer watched her walk away.

"You have a hell of a woman there that obviously loves you a lot," Kelvin said.

"Yeah, she's something special," Summer murmured. "I love her more than I've ever loved anything in my life."

India smiled and hugged her.

"I thought she was going to kill Rob," Pierre exclaimed.

Everyone laughed.

~

Over the next few weeks, Brandt and Bean worked together to cast the new movie, and they also made a couple of trips to Vancouver to approve the set design for the studio and get the permits from the city to shoot the scenes on the beach and in the park. This caused Brandt to miss two of the shows, which Summer wasn't happy about, especially after everything that had gone down with Rob.

Summer had rehearsed some days until she was so tired she could barely make the drive out to Santa Monica, but she and Rob had remained in the top two of the leader board each week and only had two more weeks to go. He wasn't exactly cordial, but Summer made him work so hard he barely had any breath to say anything stupid, and when he did, she changed the routine to make it even harder for him. After a few days, he'd finally learned to keep his big mouth shut. She was ready for Brandt to be home. It was lonely without her in the big house, which was why she'd chosen to work twice as hard over the past few weeks.

"I'm so glad the finale is next week, then I can put this season behind me. Balancing on the door of the closet is making me crazy. I don't know what to do and I'm scared. I'm sure once the season ends that dickhead will out me to the whole world and ruin my career," Summer said into the phone. She was curled up on the couch watching TV. She still had a couple of days before Brandt was supposed to return.

"I know this isn't easy. I'm behind you with whatever you do," Brandt replied.

"Thanks. How's the movie going? Did you get everything ready to start filming?"

"We had to pull some strings to get around an ordinance, but we finally got our permit. We start filming the week after next."

"That's good. The last time, you filmed throughout my whole show."

"I know it. Maybe you can come up there for a little bit."

"That actually sounds like fun. I've never watched a movie being filmed," Summer exclaimed.

"It's not as cool as it sounds. It's actually kind of boring, but I'd love to have you with me. This isn't one of my films, so I won't be there the entire time, which means I'll get more time with you."

"We have to do the ten city tour after the show ends, so that'll take up three weeks of my time. I'll join you in Vancouver when it's over."

"Sounds great."

"Yeah. Can I fast forward to the end of those three weeks?" Summer sighed. "These last couple of weeks haven't been great, so I'm sure the next four won't be any better."

"How is he behaving?"

"It hasn't been too bad. I've had him so busy he can barely keep up."

"It's the finale of the show and you're one of the front runners for the second season in a row. You love this and you need to have a great time doing what you love, despite that asshat."

Summer smiled. "I know. I actually choreographed what I think are some of my best routines ever. Still, Pierre and I are on pins and needles until Rob opens his mouth. You know, I thought it was easier for gay men, but he's as nervous as a mouse in a room full of traps," she said.

"It's not easy for anyone, especially when they can't come out on their own terms. It's a lot different when the person decides to come out and chooses the time and day to do it. They've had time to digest what is happening and think about how it will affect them. Look at all of the celebrities that have come out over the years—they've all done it themselves and weren't outed by some bigoted piece of garbage."

"I know," Summer murmured.

"It sounds like you could use a hug," Brandt said.

"Yeah. I miss you."

"Then open the door," Brandt stated.

"What?" Summer questioned as she got up and walked over to the front of the house. "Brandt!" she exclaimed, jumping into her arms when she pulled the door open. "I thought you weren't coming home until Friday."

"Well, I'll leave if you want," Brandt teased, holding her tightly.

"No way!" Summer replied, kissing her.

"Congratulations on making it into the finale. I'm sorry I missed the last two shows." Brandt grabbed her bag and walked inside with her arm around Summer's waist.

"Thank you, and it's okay. I know you have to travel. It doesn't bother me. Although, it's a little spooky around here when you're not home."

"What do you mean?" Brandt asked, walking up the stairs to change her clothes and unpack.

"Things go bump in the night."

Brandt laughed. "I've lived here for the last six years...alone. All houses make a little noise, but I can promise you, this house isn't haunted."

"What about the three years you were with your ex?"

Brandt took off her shoes and walked out of the closet where Summer was sitting on the bench in front of the bed.

"I haven't lived with anyone since my freshman year of college."

"Seriously?"

Brandt nodded.

"But you were engaged."

Brandt shrugged. "We weren't living together." She sat down next to Summer. "We both traveled a lot, but we probably would've seen each other more if we'd lived together. I guess it wasn't meant to be." She leaned over, kissing Summer softly, before wrapping her arm around her waist.

"Do you think you'll ever attempt to get married again?" Summer murmured, laying her head on Brandt's shoulder. It was a subject they hadn't really talked about since the cruise, and with everything Brandt had gone through the first time around, she wasn't sure if it was something she even wanted.

"I don't want to go through a big wedding again, no," Brandt sighed as she stood to finish changing clothes.

"What about going to Vegas? They do all the work for you."

"That's not a bad idea," Brandt laughed, popping her head out of the closet. Summer was looking directly at her with an expression she hadn't seen before. "Are you serious?" she asked, stepping closer to her.

"Yes. I want to spend the rest of my life with you, and I want it to start this weekend," Summer stated with a smile.

"Wow, I..." Brandt fumbled, slightly speechless. She thought about the upcoming weekend. "There's something about the third, isn't there?"

Summer grinned. "That's the day I spilled my coffee on you."

"It's already been a year?" Brandt shook her head, realizing it was also nearly a year since the worst day of her life happened, but the best thing in her life was also sitting right in front of her, asking her to spend the rest of their lives together.

Brandt looked into the pale green eyes staring back at her. She walked closer, kneeling in front of Summer and taking her hands. "If you want to spend the rest of your life as my wife, there's nothing I could ever want more. I love you, Summer." She smiled.

"So, that's a yes?" Summer squealed, throwing her arms around Brandt when she nodded. They shared a passionate kiss before Brandt pulled back slightly.

"Are you sure you want to go to Vegas?"

"Yes. I'd never make you go through a big wedding again."

"What about your family?" Brandt asked.

"You're all that matters to me. I'll send them pictures and they can meet you when things slow down for both of us. My mother and sister know about you, so it's not like it'll be a huge surprise."

"Really?"

"I told them the truth when I went home for the holidays and they asked me about the articles in the tabloids. Does your family know?"

"Yes. They know I'm dating someone and it's serious."

"Okay then, let's book a flight and get ready to go," Summer said excitedly.

"Alright." Brandt smiled. "What are you going to wear?"

"I have this platinum-colored dress that I love." Summer held it up. The top was beaded and off the shoulders, and the bottom skirt was chiffon. "Will it work as a wedding dress though?"

"Sure. It's beautiful. I think I have a platinum-colored necktie that will go with it."

"I like it when you wear a black suit with a black shirt and then a colored tie—unless you're wearing a vest and bowtie, of course. I really like that look."

"I only have black and wine colored bow tie sets, but I can wear black on black with the platinum tie."

"That sounds good," Summer said.

"What about rings?"

"We can stop at a jewelry store on the way to the airport. I'm sure we'll find something we like," Summer beamed as she began packing.

Brandt nodded with a smile and went into her office to book the flight and the hotel. She walked back into the bedroom a few minutes later. "Our flight leaves an hour and a half after you finish rehearsal, so I'll take you there in the morning and pick you up on the way to the airport."

"That'll work out great."

Brandt picked Summer up, spinning her around. "We're going to Vegas to get married!" she squealed.

Summer laughed and kissed her.

Chapter 30

The next afternoon, Brandt and Summer arrived at their hotel and headed up to their room.

"I called ahead this morning and booked our ceremony for this evening at sunset in the floral garden. The efficient will be here twenty minutes before to go over everything and there will also be a photographer. The only thing we need to do now is go get the license."

"Wow, you were busy this morning." Summer smiled.

Brandt set their suitcase down and hung the garment bag in the closet. "I figured these places probably fill up, and I was right. I had to pay a little extra, but it's just a short and simple ceremony with only the two of us, so there wasn't much for them to put together. We're actually being squeezed in between two already scheduled weddings."

Summer shook her head and laughed as they headed back into the elevator to catch a cab over to the clerk of courts.

~

That evening, as the sky burst into multiple colors from the setting sun, Brandt and Summer stood together, hand in hand in front of a balding, older gentleman, saying their vows to each other as another man stood a few feet away, snapping pictures. The ceremony was quick, and the photographer took a few intimate shots of the two of them in the gardens before leaving them alone with a promise to deliver the CD of the photos to the hotel before their flight out the next morning.

Brandt looked down at the platinum band on her left hand with small, recessed diamonds. "We did it!" she said, with a big smile. "I love you, Summer Coghlan!" she added, shaking her head. "I still can't believe you dropped your last name and took mine."

Summer grinned, wrapping her arms around Brandt. "I love you, and I want everyone to know it."

The platinum band full of diamonds on her left hand sparkled in the light as they made their way back inside of the hotel. The employees at the desk rang a bell and cheered as they walked across the lobby. Summer and Brandt smiled and waved as they hurried into the elevator.

As soon as they entered their room, they noticed a tray of fresh, chocolate-covered strawberries and a nice bottle of chilled champagne awaited them in the sitting area. Summer pulled Brandt's tie loose and began unbuttoning her shirt as she shimmied out of her jacket and pulled off her shoes. Summer turned around for Brandt to unzip her dress.

"I want to be naked with you," Summer murmured, as they peeled out of their clothes.

Brandt opened the champagne and poured two glasses, then she carried the tray over to the nightstand next to the bed. Summer pulled the blanket and sheet back and crawled into the middle. Brandt climbed in next to her, handing Summer one of the glasses. They toasted their marriage and drank a few sips before devouring the strawberries, and then each other, making love most of the night.

~

The next morning, Summer was just waking up when Brandt walked into the room, pushing the tray of full of room service she'd ordered for breakfast.

"Good morning, Mrs. Coghlan," Brandt grinned, leaning down to kiss her.

"Right back at you," Summer yawned. "Something smells good."

"Well, I did take a shower, but you're probably referring to the breakfast cart." Brandt smiled. "I wasn't sure what you'd want, so I ordered a bunch of different things."

Summer's stomach growled loudly when she sat up and pulled on the robe draped over the couch. "We skipped dinner didn't we?"

"Yeah, we had reservations, but you wanted to go right to desert."

"I do seem to recall you initiating it as much as I did." Summer grinned, walking over to check out the food on the cart. She set a few of the plates on the coffee table in front of the couch before sitting down.

"Either way, we consummated the marriage, so it's official." Brandt sat down next to her and picked up a fork. "I got the disc the photographer left, by the way."

"Did you look at it?" Summer asked with a mouthful of pancakes.

Brandt laughed. "Yeah, the guy at the desk let me review it. They came out great."

Summer nodded.

"Our flight leaves in three hours, so we have plenty of time to eat and for you to shower before we have to head to the airport."

"Sounds like we have a little more time than that," Summer teased.

Brandt shook her head and laughed. "I was thinking after your tour ends and I finish with this movie—let's go on a proper honeymoon."

"Yes, definitely," Summer replied. "What are you thinking about?"

"Warm and tropical maybe," Brandt suggested.

"I don't care where we go, as long as I'm with you. It's always an adventure." Summer smiled and leaned over, kissing her softly.

Brandt set her fork down and pushed Summer to her back, crawling on top of her.

~

Summer and Brandt nearly missed their flight home, which only added to the excitement of the weekend. On Monday morning, Brandt was sitting in her office trying to get caught up on some paperwork when Bean walked in and plopped down on the chair in front of her desk.

"I narrowed those scripts down over the weekend. There are about six or seven good ones and at least three, maybe four that I feel will be great movies. I thought my eyes were going to pop out." Bean shook her head. "What did you do all weekend?"

"Summer and I went to Vegas."

"What for?" Bean furrowed her brow. "I thought you were excited to be home after traveling over the last couple of weeks."

"I was, but one thing led to another," Brandt said, holding up her left hand so that the back of it was facing Bean and the diamonds in her wedding band glistened.

"Oh, my God, you didn't." Bean shook her head.

"I did."

"Why didn't you tell me?"

"It happened so fast, my head is still spinning."

"Wow. Brandt Coghlan, a married woman!" Bean jumped up and ran around the desk to hug her best friend. "I'm happy for you. I'm pissed I wasn't there and you didn't tell me, but I honestly couldn't be happier. Summer's a good person and she's beautiful."

"Thank you. I'm sorry you weren't there. I thought of calling you, but I didn't want you to fly out at the last minute for a ten-minute ceremony." Brandt bumped the mouse on her laptop and brought up the disc full of pictures. "Here, look at these."

"Oh, wow. You two look great. Where is this at?"

"Why? Are you thinking of taking Misty?" Brandt teased, before telling her the name of the hotel.

"No. What we have is casual and works out great."

"You know what the best thing is? I married someone I am head over heels in love with and it cost me a small fraction of the price I paid for the wedding that didn't happen with a person I wasn't in love with."

"I always say everything happens for a reason." Bean grinned.

Summer worked late Monday and Tuesday night, prepping for the finale of the show. Brandt had barely seen her wife in the few days that they'd been married. She and Bean arrived a little early for the live performance but were unable to see Summer since they were already working on camera blocking and dress rehearsals. Bean was thrilled to be sitting in the front row.

The show started with the full troupe doing the Bachata, then the pairs came out for their first dance, which was the voter's choice. Summer and Rob were voted to do the Rumba, which neither of them were happy with, but they had to do it. The sexy Latin dance was full of slow, intimate moves, bringing their bodies together time and time again, with short, quick steps pulling them apart, before the sultry music brought them back together again.

Brandt hated seeing the shirtless monster, Rob, handling Summer like a lover as they moved through the dance. She couldn't deny the fact that the routine was beautiful. It had melted her heart all over again watching Summer perform the dance. She looked like an angel in a white, sheer and chiffon wrap that covered her breasts and one side but left the other side and hip open, as well as one leg. The costume resembled that of a bed sheet tangled around a lover.

When the song ended, Summer and Rob were called to the middle of the floor by the host of the show to speak with them before the break.

"I think that was your best dance yet this season," the host said with a smile.

"Aww, thank you. Rob worked very hard to get that choreography down," Summer replied.

"I'm looking forward to our freestyle. I think Summer really outdid herself with that one. I thought I'd never get the steps down." Rob smiled.

"I know you both need to get back and get ready for the next performance, but Summer, I heard you did something exciting over the weekend," he stated.

"Besides rehearsing with my amazing dance partner?" She grinned. "Yes, I did actually. I married my amazingly talented wife, Brandt Coghlan."

Bean gasped and Brandt simply smiled when the camera closest to them spun around to face their direction. The crowd cheered and clapped loudly.

"I know I'm not the first, but I want to say congratulations. I wish you both all the best," the host added.

The show cut to a commercial and Summer ran back stage to get ready for her troupe routine while Rob moseyed back there like a kid that fell in the mud. The look on his face was priceless, and Summer loved every minute of it.

Pierre, India, and Kelvin surrounded Summer, hugging her and congratulating her. Rob walked up to say something, but Kelvin stepped in front of him, letting him know that if he messed with her, then he messed with the entire troupe. Rob walked away to get ready for his next dance without saying a word.

~

"I can't believe she just outed herself on live TV," Bean whispered.

"I can." Brandt smiled.

As soon as the commercial ended, the show continued with another troupe dance, then more of the pair dancing, and so on until they were down to the final half hour, which had a performance by a chart-topping musician, and a few more troupe dances, followed by the results of the live show.

The host stepped into the center of the dance floor with the three pairs. He started with the third-place pair, who bowed when the crowd cheered, then stepped to the side. Pierre and Summer were the final two pros, so they stood together with their partners on their opposite sides.

"The winners of season two of *Anyone Can Dance* are Rob and Summer!" the host exclaimed as confetti rained from the ceiling.

The audience cheered so loud Brandt barely heard them cut the end of the show. All of the pros gathered around and Pierre and Kelvin picked Summer up on their shoulders. Brandt and Bean screamed and clapped with everyone around them as they watched the celebration. When Summer was back on her feet, she found her way through the other dancers to the edge of the dance floor where Brandt was sitting and flew into her open arms.

"I'm so proud of you!" Brandt cheered, kissing her and holding her tight.

"I love you!" Summer yelled before going back into the pile of people on the dance floor.

~

The next morning, Summer had appeared on the *Today Show* with Rob to perform part of one of their winning dances and talk about the show. When she was asked about her new marriage, Summer kept it short and sweet, telling them she was over the moon with happiness.

Brandt was on the side of the set, watching with Pierre and India since they'd invited all three of the top teams to the show.

"I feel so liberated," Summer announced when she and Brandt boarded the plane to fly back to L.A. from New York. "It's like being freed from prison."

"I hope you didn't marry me so you could come out of the closet," Brandt teased.

Summer rolled her head to the side and smiled. "I married you because you make me the happiest person in the world and I love you with all of my heart." She grinned. "Spilling the coffee on you, then rear-ending you were obviously meant to be because they brought me to you."

"What if I hadn't gone on my honeymoon cruise?"

"We would've run into each other again somewhere else. We frequented a few of the same cafés and restaurants because your office and my rehearsal studio for the show are near each other. It was bound to happen eventually." Summer smiled.

Brandt leaned over, kissing her softly as the plane took off.

~

As soon as they landed in California, they turned their phones back on. Summer had three missed calls from the producer of *Anyone Can Dance*, so she quickly called him back as they made their way out of the airport with paparazzi taking photos.

"I just landed. Is everything okay?" she asked.

"It's more than okay. Have you seen social media and the internet?" he exclaimed.

"No. I'm kind of scared to," she laughed.

"You're trending at number one right now and have been all morning. That's why I was calling you. We're extending your contract from two years to five years and adding in more choreography responsibility. I need you to swing by the production office sometime today."

"Wow. Alright. I'll be there soon." Summer hung up and looked at Brandt as they headed to her car.

"What's going on?"

"Apparently, I'm extremely popular at the moment. They're extending my contract."

"That's great." Brandt grabbed her hand and leaned over to kiss her as they walked.

When they got into the car, Brandt's phone started ringing. She checked the caller ID and noticed it was one of her friends that was also a producer.

"Hey, Bernie. What's up?"

"Harris tried to call Summer, but I'm not if he had the correct number and well, since the buzz going around says she's your new wife, is there any chance I can speak with her?" he said.

"Sure," Brandt laughed. "It's for you," she said handing Summer the phone.

Summer talked and listened, then talked again while Brandt drove them through the city and out towards their house in the mountains of Santa Monica. Summer finally hung up when Brandt was driving through their gate.

"What was that about?" she asked.

"They want to hire me to choreograph all of the dancing for a movie they're producing. It's a true story about a street dancer turned ballroom pro."

"Wow. Really? That's great, Summer."

Summer looked down at the phone in her hand and laughed.

"What?" Brandt asked.

"Nothing, just thinking about everything that I've been through in the past year, with you of course," she replied, getting out of the car.

"You were so worried you'd lose everything," Brandt said, squeezing her hand as they walked inside.

"Instead, I've gained so much more," Summer murmured, wrapping her arms around Brandt's neck. "It's like it all happened for a reason."

"That's because it was meant to be." Brandt grinned, kissing her softly.

About the Author

Graysen Morgen is the bestselling author of *Falling Snow*, *Fast Pitch*, *Cypress Lake*, and the Bridal Series: *Bridesmaid of Honor* and *Brides*, as well as many other titles. She was born and raised in North Florida with winding rivers and waterways at her back door and the white sandy beach a mile away. She has spent most of her lifetime in the sun and on the water. She enjoys reading, writing, fishing, and spending as much time as possible with her wife and their daughter.

You can contact Graysen at graysenmorgen@aol.com; like her fan page on facebook.com/graysenmorgen; and follow her on twitter @graysenmorgen

Other Titles Available From
Triplicity Publishing

Coming Home by Graysen Morgen. After tragedy derails TJ Abernathy's life, she packs up her three year old son and heads back to Pennsylvania to live with her grandmother on the family farm. TJ picks back up where she left off eight years earlier, tending to the fruit and nut tree orchard, while learning her grandmother's secret trade. Soon, TJ's high school sweetheart and the same girl who broke her heart, comes back into her life, threatening to steal it away once again. As the weeks turn into months and tragedy strikes again, TJ realizes coming home was the best thing she could've ever done.

Special Assignment by Austen Thorne. Secret Service Agent Parker Meeks has her hands full when she gets her new assignment, protecting a Congressman's teenage daughter, who has had threats made on her life and been whisked away to a Christian boarding school under an alias to finish out her senior year. Parker is fine with the assignment, until she finds out she has to go undercover as a Canon Priest. The last thing Parker expects to find is a beautiful, art history teacher, who is intrigued by her in more ways than one.

Miracle at Christmas by Sydney Canyon. A Modern Twist on the Classic Scrooge Story. Dylan is a power-hungry lawyer who pushed away everything good in her life to become the best defense attorney in the, often winning the worst cases and keeping anyone with enough money out of jail. She's visited on Christmas Eve by her deceased law partner, who threatens her with a life in hell like his own, if she doesn't change her path. During the course of the night, she is taken on a journey through her past, present, and future with three very different spirits.

Bella Vita by Sydney Canyon. Brady is the First Officer of the crew on the *Bella Vita*, a luxury charter yacht in the Caribbean. She enjoys the laidback island lifestyle, and is accustomed to high profile guests, but when a U.S. Senator charters the yacht as a gift to his beautiful twin daughters who have just graduated from college and a few of their friends, she literally has her hands full.

Brides *(Bridal Series book 2)* by Graysen Morgen. Britton Prescott is dating the love of her life, Daphne Attwood, after a few tumultuous events that happened to unravel at her sister's wedding reception, seven months earlier. She's happy with the way things are, but immense pressure from her family and friends to take the next step, nearly sends her back to the single life. The idea of a long engagement and simple wedding are thrown out the window, as both families take over, rushing Britton and Daphne to the altar in a matter of weeks.

Cypress Lake by Graysen Morgen. The small town of Cypress Lake is rocked when one murder after another happens. Dani Ricketts, the Chief Deputy for the Cypress Lake Sheriff's Office, realizes the murders are linked. She's surprised when the girl that broke her heart in high school has not only returned home, but she's also Dani's only suspect. Kristen Malone has come back to Cypress Lake to put the past behind her so that she can move on with her life. Seeing Dani Ricketts again throws her off-guard, nearly derailing her plans to finally rid herself and her family of Cypress Lake.

Crashing Waves by Graysen Morgen. After a tragic accident, Pro Surfer, Rory Eden, spends her days hiding in the surf and snowboard manufacturing company that she built from the ground up, while living her life as a shell of the person that she once was. Rory's world is turned upside when a young surfer pursues her, asking for the one thing she can't do. Adler Troy and Dr. Cason Macauley from Graysen Morgen's best seller, *Falling Snow,* make an appearance in this romantic adventure about life, love, and letting go.

Bridesmaid of Honor *(Bridal Series book 1)* by Graysen Morgen. Britton Prescott's best friend is getting married and she's the maid of honor. As if that isn't enough to deal with, Britton's sister announces she's getting married in the same month and her maid of honor is her best friend Daphne, the same woman who has tormented Britton for years. Britton has to suck it up and play nice, instead of scratching her eyes out, because she and Daphne are in both weddings. Everyone is counting on them to behave like adults.

Falling Snow by Graysen Morgen. Dr. Cason Macauley, a high-speed trauma surgeon from Denver meets Adler Troy, a professional snowboarder and sparks fly. The last thing Cason wants is a relationship and Adler doesn't realize what's right in front of her until it's gone, but will it be too late?

Fate vs. Destiny by Graysen Morgen. Logan Greer devotes her life to investigating plane crashes for the National Transportation Safety Board. Brooke McCabe is an investigator with the Federal Aviation Association who literally flies by the seat of her pants. When Logan gets tangled in head games with both women will she choose fate or destiny?

Just Me by Graysen Morgen. Wild child Ian Wiley has to grow up and take the reins of the hundred year old family business when tragedy strikes. Cassidy Harland is a little surprised that she came within an inch of picking up a gorgeous stranger in a bar and is shocked to find out that stranger is the new head of her company.

Love Loss Revenge by Graysen Morgen. Rian Casey is an FBI Agent working the biggest case of her career and madly in love with her girlfriend. Her world is turned upside when tragedy strikes. Heartbroken, she tries to rebuild her life. When she discovers the truth behind what really happened that awful night she decides justice isn't good enough, and vows revenge on everyone involved.

Natural Instinct by Graysen Morgen. Chandler Scott is a Marine Biologist who keeps her private life private. Corey Joslen is intrigued by Chandler from the moment she meets her. Chandler is forced to finally open her life up to Corey. It backfires in Corey's face and sends her running. Will either woman learn to trust her natural instinct?

Secluded Heart by Graysen Morgen. Chase Leery is an overworked cardiac surgeon with a group of best friends that have an opinion and a reason for everything. When she meets a new artist named Remy Sheridan at her best friend's art gallery she is captivated by the reclusive woman. When Chase finds out why Remy is so sheltered will she put her career on the line to help her or is it too difficult to love someone with a secluded heart?

In Love, at War by Graysen Morgen. Charley Hayes is in the Army Air Force and stationed at Ford Island in Pearl Harbor. She is the commanding officer of her own female-only service squadron and doing the one thing she loves most, repairing airplanes. Life is good for Charley, until the day she finds herself falling in love while fighting for her life as her country is thrown haphazardly into World War II. Can she survive being in love and at war?

Fast Pitch by Graysen Morgen. Graham Cahill is a senior in college and the catcher and captain of the softball team. Despite being an all-star pitcher, Bailey Michaels is young and arrogant. Graham and Bailey are forced to get to know each other off the field in order to learn to work together on the field. Will the extra time pay off or will it drive a nail through the team?

Submerged by Graysen Morgen. Assistant District Attorney Layne Carmichael had no idea that the sexy woman she took home from a local bar for a one night stand would turn out to be someone she would be prosecuting months later. Scooter is a Naval Officer on a submarine who changes women like she changes uniforms. When she is accused of a heinous crime she is shocked to see her latest conquest sitting across from her as the prosecuting attorney.

Vow of Solitude by Austen Thorne. Detective Jordan Denali is in a fight for her life against the ghosts from her past and a Serial Killer taunting her with his every move. She lives a life of solitude and plans to keep it that way. When Callie Marceau, a curious Medical Examiner, decides she wants in on the biggest case of her career, as well as, Jordan's life, Jordan is powerless to stop her.

Igniting Temptation by Sydney Canyon. Mackenzie Trotter is the Head of Pediatrics at the local hospital. Her life takes a rather unexpected turn when she meets a flirtatious, beautiful fire fighter. Both women soon discover it doesn't take much to ignite temptation.

One Night by Sydney Canyon. While on a business trip, Caylen Jarrett spends an amazing night with a beautiful stripper. Months later, she is shocked and confused when that same woman re-enters her life. The fact that this stranger could destroy her career doesn't bother her. C.J. is more terrified of the feelings this woman stirs in her. Could she have fallen in love in one night and not even known it?

Fine by Sydney Can
yon. Collin Anderson hides behind a façade, pretending everything is fine. Her workaholic wife and best friend are both oblivious as she goes on an emotional journey, battling a potentially hereditary disease that her mother has been diagnosed with. The only person who knows what is really going on, is Collin's doctor. The same

doctor, who is an acquaintance that she's always been attracted to, and who has a partner of her own.

Shadow's Eyes by Sydney Canyon. Tyler McCain is the owner of a large ranch that breeds and sells different types of horses. She isn't exactly thrilled when a Hollywood movie producer shows up wanting to film his latest movie on her property. Reegan Delsol is an up and coming actress who has everything going for her when she lands the lead role in a new film, but there one small problem that could blow the entire picture.

Light Reading: A Collection of Novellas by Sydney Canyon. Four of Sydney Canyon's novellas together in one book, including the bestsellers *Shadow's Eyes* and *One Night*.

Visit us at www.tri-pub.com

Made in the USA
Lexington, KY
05 September 2017